He was hot—for her!

Eva's cheeks were flushed, her blue eyes snapped and she'd spent nearly the whole hour tempting him. Her sweater had all but slipped off one shoulder, exposing smooth, sexy skin.

He better go home before he did something stupid. Like kiss her. Or more.

"Actually—" he glanced at his watch "—I should call it a night."

Then he turned to smile and kiss her cheek in a platonic good-night.

Come on, Ames. Get the hell out while you can.

"I had fun, Eva." He reached for the door handle. "Thanks for— What are you *doing?*"

"Who, me?" She'd swung her crazily booted leg over both of his and had managed to straddle him in the cab. "I'm just saying you're welcome, Ames."

"Jeez, you can't—"

Yes, she could. She was already kissing him, hot, hungry kisses, pressing her body close.

He was a guy. That got a reaction. A fairly immediate and large one.

Wait, there was some reason he was going to avoid getting physical with her. Now he couldn't remember what it was. In fact, his hands were at her waist, traveling down to explore the pink skirt.

Oh, man.

Blaze®

Dear Reader,

I had so much fun writing *Some Like It Hotter* and playing with New York/California stereotypes to create a story of contrasts. I grew up in central New Jersey, and my husband is from California, so we are well aware that not everyone in New York is driven and harsh, and not everyone in California is a surfer dude, but those types served my story theme and provided a lot of fun, so I didn't flinch.

Eva Meyer and her twin sister, Chris, learn a lot about themselves by switching coasts, coffee shops and lives. I hope you enjoy Eva's experience trading a tiny West Coast town for the nonstop thrill ride of New York City. And I hope in February you'll look for her sister's story, in which former New Yorker Chris tries to cope with the slow pace of life in California and too many hot men!

Cheers,

Isabel Sharpe

www.IsabelSharpe.com

Some Like It Hotter

—

Isabel Sharpe

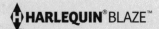

HARLEQUIN® BLAZE™

Recycling programs
for this product may
not exist in your area.

ISBN-13: 978-0-373-79820-9

SOME LIKE IT HOTTER

Printed in U.S.A.

www.Harlequin.com

ABOUT THE AUTHOR

Isabel Sharpe was not born with pen in hand like so many of her fellow writers. After she quit work to stay home with her firstborn son and nearly went out of her mind, she started writing. After more than thirty novels for Harlequin, a second son and eventually a new, improved husband, Isabel is more than happy with her choices these days. She loves hearing from readers. Write to her at www.isabelsharpe.com.

Books by Isabel Sharpe

HARLEQUIN BLAZE

376—MY WILDEST RIDE
393—INDULGE ME
444—NO HOLDING BACK
533—WHILE SHE WAS SLEEPING…
539—SURPRISE ME…
595—TURN UP THE HEAT
606—LONG SLOW BURN
619—HOT TO THE TOUCH
678—JUST ONE KISS
704—LIGHT ME UP
714—FEELS SO RIGHT
761—HALF-HITCHED
771—BACK IN SERVICE
792—NOTHING TO HIDE

Other titles by this author available in ebook format.

To get the inside scoop on Harlequin Blaze and its talented writers, be sure to check out blazeauthors.com.

To Paul Miller and Lissy Matthews of Colectivo Coffee, who helped me tremendously by answering all my pesky java questions.

Prologue

THE SUN WAS setting over the Pacific. Eva Meyer sat on Aura Beach on California's Central Coast, a cup of her own blend of orange chamomile tea in hand. The colors were fantastic, a soaring ceiling of pink, orange and burgundy, reflected in the clouds and across the water. Over her cheeks blew a gentle, fresh September breeze. Pelicans winged past, long necks doubled back, wings arcing, heading south. Any moment the magic of a dolphin breaching the ocean's restless surface could happen.

She was bored stiff.

As a matter of fact, she'd been feeling off center and uncharacteristically low for the past several months. Around here they'd put her funk down to some interruption in her chi or planets out of alignment or angry spirits or whatever mystical forces might be at work—but her sensible midwestern roots were looking for a more concrete reason. Maybe she'd been working too hard, maybe she hadn't been social enough, *definitely* she hadn't been getting enough sex. But boredom? That kind of thing wasn't easy to admit. Only the Boring Get Bored had been her accountant mother's mantra, which Eva had lived by—often to an excess her mother didn't approve of.

But today, during this relatively rare moment of relaxation and reflection, the ugly truth had burst from its hiding place and smacked her across the face.

Ow.

For the past three of her twenty-eight years she'd been the proud owner of the Slow Pour coffee shop in the tiny town of Carmia, building a decent business, honing its identity, growing its reputation. Though she totally loved the shop, loved the friendly vibe it put out in the community for residents and tourists alike, was totally into the challenge of keeping the business afloat, underneath it all she was…

Bored.

How could this happen? Years of learning beside her father, coffee scientist Dr. Meyer, decades of traveling to major coffee-producing locations—Hawaii, Ethiopia, Brazil, Indonesia—had fostered her dream. All her life she'd known she'd escape the Midwest for the serenity, beauty and open-mindedness of the California coast, that she'd be her own boss with her own shop…she was living a fantasy come true! How many people got to do that?

Her fraternal twin sister, Chris, older by a whole two minutes and as glamorous and driven as Eva was nonconformist and laid-back, had made her same dream come true in New York City, buying the shop NYEspresso a couple of years after Eva rescued a sad little bankrupt souvenir shop and transformed it into Slow Pour. You didn't see *Chris* whining after achieving her life's goal. What kind of spoiled brat would have it all and still be wanting more?

She sighed, sipping her tea, watching the sky turn Crayola colors…

Bored.

"UNGH." CHRIS FLOPPED onto the narrow bed in her small bedroom in the tiny apartment on East Eighty-Seventh

Street that she shared with her roommate, Natalie. Outside her window a siren blared, horns honked, a driver shouted, "Get the heck out of the way, please!"

Only he didn't say *please.* Or *heck.*

She was exhausted.

Not fun to admit. Or to experience. She'd always had the energy of an ant. Or a hummingbird. Or a gazelle. Now she was more like a cow. Or cat. Or sloth. For a while she thought maybe her low mood was due to the death of her favorite season, summer, and the approaching long winter months. Or maybe residual disappointment over her breakup with John, though that had been weeks ago, and they'd only dated four months before realizing they were not so meant to be after all.

But today she'd actually turned down an invitation to go dancing with friends from her Zumba class. Instead, she'd chosen to come home, eat a bowl of soup and stare at the wall, because she was…

Exhausted.

No, no, this was all wrong! Since when did anything even slow her down, let alone wear her out? She'd known her whole life that she'd end up in a major city someday. Noise, bustle and a certain amount of chaos were her bread and butter, her peanut butter and Nutella, her French roast and cream. Bright lights, big city—oh, yeah, bring it on! And had she ever. For the past three years, she'd been part of the amazing ride that was New York City, working first as a manager at Fine Grind and last year buying the store and making it her own, NYEspresso. She hadn't been turning an amazing profit, but hadn't run it into the ground, either. Her dream had come true! Somebody pinch her!

No, someone *punch* her for all this whining. Her free-spirited twin, Eva, had also achieved coffee nirvana, and she was having a blast, not a boohoo-fest.

Chris lifted her head, gave up, let it drop back on the pillow.

Nothing helped. She was simply…

Exhausted.

THE SUN'S GLOWING disk disappeared over the horizon. Eva hauled her cell out of her pocket to call her sister. Born on Christmas Eve—hence their names—on the surface Chris and Eva were about as different as two souls could be, except for their shared love of all things coffee. But they still had the deep bond of most twins. Chris might not understand Eva's off mood, but she'd be supportive and helpful, even if it was just to tell Eva to snap out of it.

Maybe that was all Eva needed.

Chris picked up immediately. "Hey, twin, how goes it?"

"Okay." Eva frowned. "What's wrong? You don't sound like yourself."

"You don't sound like yourself, either."

"No? Who do I sound like? Wait, don't tell me. Scarlett Johansson."

"I'm thinking…Eva with sharp edges. Who do I sound like?"

"Chris dulled down."

"Tell me what's going on?" They both spoke at once.

"You first."

"No, you."

Eva giggled. Just hearing her twin's voice made her feel better. "I'm sitting on warm sand watching the sky fade from magenta to coral to pink to navy. There are palm trees behind me, waves making a great swishing sound in front of me…"

Chris snorted. "And something is *wrong?*"

"I know." She grabbed a handful of sand, let it flow through her fingers. "I'm restless, not feeling peaceful. Been this way for a while, just something not quite right."

"Time for new hair?"

Eva grinned at their joke girlie remedy for whatever was wrong. "I bought a ton of new accessories to decorate it with. Didn't help."

"Accessories? I'm afraid to ask what these are like." Her sister made a shuddering noise. "Is Slow Pour doing well?"

"Not great, not bad."

"Man trouble?"

"No man to cause any."

"Ha. Maybe *that's* your problem."

Eva snorted. "Could be. What's been going on with you?"

Her sister sighed. "I don't know. Just…lethargy."

"I can't picture that at all. You're usually a blur of a person."

"I feel like I need a change."

"Me, too." Eva pulled her hoodie closer as the air chilled with the fading light. "I moved to California because it's so laid-back, but sometimes it feels like nothing happens, and the nothing that happens does it really slowly."

"That sounds like heaven." Her sister sighed. "*Everything* is *always* happening around here, all at top speed."

"That sounds like heaven." Eva lay back on the sand, looking up into the night sky, and a crazy, impractical, ridiculous thought made her giggle.

"What's so funny?"

"Since we can't leave our shops to go on an extended

vacation—maybe we should just switch lives for a month."

Silence. Then both sisters gasped. "Oh, my God!"

_1_

"CHRIS! I'M HERE. I'm calling from your apartment!" Eva dumped her bags in Chris's tiny foyer, which wasn't really more than the beginning of a narrow hallway. She'd visited her sister only once in New York, shortly after Chris moved here. Generally they saw each other in Wisconsin when they got together with their parents for the holidays.

"Let me guess. It's much bigger than you remember." Chris's voice dripped sarcasm.

"Uh…not really." Eva peeked around a corner toward the kitchen, the size of her closet, and the living room, which struggled to contain a chair, love seat and coffee table. "But it's got so much charm!"

"Oh, is that charm? I thought charm was your house, with the plants and flowers growing everywhere and the ocean smell outside. Try and see how charming my place is in February when it's dark and freezing for weeks on end. I can actually run from one end of your place to another. Run! It's a real house!"

"A tiny house. Which you have to take care of." She hoisted her bags again, phone between her chin and ear, and marched down the hall, then pushed open the first door. "Your bedroom is adorable."

"You can barely turn around—you call that adorable? I can do jumping jacks in yours! I can see an expanse of floor! And then I can take a dozen steps and be *outside!* And to the *beach* in five minutes! No elevator, no sirens, no taxis, no—"

"Concerts or museums, no theater, no—"

"Traffic jams, no hurricanes, no impatient rude people—"

"No excitement! No energy!"

"No Ames!"

"Huh?" Eva hauled her suitcase onto the twin bed. "Who's Ames?"

Chris made a noise of exasperation. "A regular at NYEspresso. Also an arrogant pain in the ass who doesn't seem to hear me when I tell him I'm not interested. He's this complete rich-boy spoiled brat who's never heard 'no' in his life."

Eva chuckled. Men came after Chris pretty regularly. All she had to do was green-light the ones she wanted and ta-da, she had a boyfriend. Eva's quirks meant it was usually the other way around for her—she'd see someone and go after *him*. So far neither approach had worked long-term for the sisters, but they were happy to keep trying. "I'll tell him you've eloped. Maybe he'll fling himself off a building."

"Please encourage him."

"You'll have to deal with surfer dudes and lost tourists and retired hippies who order a cup of coffee and stay for hours thinking you have nothing better to do than chat. Which, sadly, you often don't. Though Zac will be there most days and he's awesome."

"So you've said. Though I still think your arrangement is weird. Who agrees to get married when they hit thirty only if nothing else works out?"

"We did." She didn't expect Chris to understand. Eva had begun to realize that while love affairs were a fabulous, fireworks-filled pleasure, when it came to choosing a life partner and future father of her children, she wasn't going to get much better than her best male friend, Zac, master's candidate at Cal Poly and regular at Slow Pour. It was precisely because they didn't burn so hot that she knew he'd be a good solid match, one that actually lasted.

But they still had a year and a half before that commitment. And as much as she adored Zac and he adored her, neither of them had yet given up hope they could find another soul mate they could also be frantic to tangle up the sheets with.

"At NYEspresso you'll have to deal with people screaming at you because you aren't moving fast enough or the line isn't moving fast enough. People act as if you're put on the planet only to serve them."

"I look forward to the challenge."

Chris giggled. "I can't believe we're doing this!"

"What, turning our hometowns into horrific stereotypes?"

"Well, yes, but I meant switching lives. Are you heading over to NYEspresso tonight?"

"Uh-huh." Eva couldn't wait to be in the place, knowing it was hers, however temporarily. "I think I can just make it over there before closing."

Chris snorted. "Yeah, figure how much time you'll need realistically, then add half an hour for delays and waiting and crowds and—"

"At least I get to *go* somewhere." At home her commute was down the hill and around a corner. Not a lot of sights to take in. "I want to meet your staff, make sure they're ready to have me take over for a month."

"They'll be thrilled. I've been such a bitch lately."

"You?" Eva scoffed. "Never!"

"Uh-huh. You take care, twin."

"You, too." Eva hung up the phone, bursting with excitement. Traffic and street noise reached her window. Civilization actually happened here—this was real life! She couldn't wait to get started. But first, deep breaths, a little meditation to get the nerves under control, calm her down so she didn't appear too frazzled when she met her crew at NYEspresso.

She sat cross-legged on the scuffed hardwood floor and closed her eyes, loosened her consciousness from her surroundings, swaying slightly to keep herself off balance, clearing her mind, trying to connect to the wise voice deep inside her that never failed to—

The apartment door burst open, making her jump. Must be Chris's roommate, new since Eva had last visited. Natalie worked near NYEspresso and had mentioned to Chris one day that she needed a roommate. According to Chris, Natalie was either trying to get into bed with a guy or getting kicked out of bed by a guy in one of the most misguided searches for love Chris had ever seen, but she was good-hearted—once she got to know you.

Eva was totally curious to meet her.

"Yeah? Well, screw *you,* Edward." Heels clunked furiously down the hallway. "Yeah? You really think that? Dream on, buddy, and guess what, you *suck* in bed."

Uh. That was not a person connected to her wise inner voice.

"No, let me tell *you,* you son-of-a— Oh. Hi." She stopped outside Eva's doorway, nearly six feet of stunning brunette, who probably weighed less than Eva, all of five-four. "I'll call you back, Edward. No? Well, fine. I won't. Ever. Up yours."

"Hi." Eva was having a hard time not giggling. Not that no one ever got pissed in Carmia, but that tirade seemed so New York to her.

"You're Chris's sister." Natalie looked Eva over curiously, taking in the turquoise ballet flats and tiered floral skirt, up to her colorful layers of loose-fitting tops, multiple ear piercings and assortment of butterfly clips in her hair. "She wasn't kidding. You're her total opposite."

"Close to it." Eva sat as tall as possible, looking Natalie over right back, from her black ankle boots over crimson leggings and black microskirt under a stylish wrapped coat with big leather fastenings, then to top it off, a wide-brimmed black hat. The epitome of fashion chic. She and Chris must turn every head in New York when they went out together.

"You meditating or something?"

"Yes." Eva smiled. "It keeps me centered and calm. You might want to—"

"Uh-huh." Natalie didn't smile back. "My stuff in the refrigerator is marked, and I need the bathroom from five to six a.m. every morning."

"Not a problem." Eva bunched her mouth to keep from smirking. *Nice to meet you, too.* "So you work for an interior design place?"

"Oh. Yeah." She said it as if it was the most boring job in the world. "I guess."

"How's that?"

"It's okay." She glanced at her watch, obviously anxious to move on.

Perversely, this made Eva want to keep her talking. "How long have you lived in New York?"

"Forever."

"Your parents, too? What did they do here?"

Her demeanor thawed a tiny bit. "Mom was a Broadway chorister. Dad is a music professor at Juilliard."

"Wow! Cool family. Are you musical?"

Natalie leaned against the doorjamb, though her body

stayed stiff. "I played clarinet for a bunch of years and took dance lessons. Had a few parts in school plays and musicals, nothing big. I still love going to shows. I probably saw all of them growing up."

"That's great." Eva studied her new roommate, wondering how much further she could pry. "So I'm sorry about the awkward conversation with Edward."

"He's a jerk. They're all jerks." Natalie shoved away from the door. "I gotta go get ready. I have a date."

"Oh." Eva frowned in confusion. "Not with Edward..."

Natalie gave her a withering stare. "As. If."

"Ah. Well, okay, then." Eva waved cheerfully. "Have fun with whoever."

Natalie stalked off.

Eva was pretty sure they'd never be best friends.

And it was a little hard to continue her meditation with her new not-best-friend crashing and muttering around the apartment, but Eva did the best she could. At least when she stood again, she felt more centered, less scattered, though still eager to get to NYEspresso.

Just under an hour later, Eva was standing outside her sister's shop on Tenth Avenue and West Forty-Third Street in the up-and-coming neighborhood of Hudson Yards. Yes, she'd misjudged how long it took to get there, but the store didn't close for an hour yet, and what a smorgasbord of faces and auras and interactions to keep her entertained during the walk and subway rides!

Around her was a population in suits, jeans and office casual, mostly denim and black, practically everyone in dark shades, and her in her wild flowery skirt and magenta hoodie. Not that anyone gave her a second glance. You could get away with pretty much any look in this town.

She pushed open the front door and was immediately

hit by her favorite smell in the world—second only to the aroma of roasting beans—freshly brewed coffee.

NYEspresso was different than she remembered, though it had been over a year since she'd visited. Chris had obviously put her own stamp on the place after buying it from the previous owners with the money she and Eva had come into at age twenty-five from wealthy grandparents on their mom's side. The space was sparer than it had been, more efficiently organized, with snappy clear plastic seats and bright white oval tables with chrome supports. The counter was also bright white, a long, sharp rectangle with ordering and cashier service at the far end and pastry behind a glass case closer to the entrance. The walls had been painted deep red and left bare except for white glass sconces surrounded by black iron cages that looked like chain mail.

Chic. Edgy. Not the most relaxing space. But this wasn't Carmia, this was Manhattan.

Eva approached the counter with a smile, held out her hand to the barista on duty, a handsome kid with three eyebrow rings and a necklace tattoo, whom she vaguely remembered had a weird nickname. "Hey, there. I'm Eva. Chris's sister."

"Yeah, hey. How are you?" Only with his thick New York accent it sounded like *Ha*-wa-*ya?* "I'm Jinx."

"Jinx, right. Just stopping in to say hi tonight. I'll be on the bar officially in the morning."

"Cool. Glad to have you. It's cool what you and Chris worked out." He looked toward the door and rolled his eyes. "Oh, brother, here we go."

Eva swung around. A large bouquet of flowers was walking toward her on male legs.

Jinx snorted. "The dude does not give up."

The flowers lowered.

Eva's heart stopped. Okay, not really—that would be ridiculous, because she'd collapse—but it sure felt as if everything inside her and in the whole world had paused to note this auspicious occasion.

Thick, short, dark hair that looked as if he'd tried hard to style it but the strands refused to lie flat. Deep brown eyes under dark brows. High cheekbones, a lean jaw. Full mouth, with a faint groove on either side. The shadow of masculine stubble. A small gold stud in one ear. Expensive dark suit, subtly patterned silk tie in blue, burgundy and beige. Gold watch. Perfectly shined shoes.

That was him. Her soul mate. Her man, her One Great Love Eternal, acronym OGLE.

Or at least he was her next hot fling.

"Chris here?" Her soul mate put the flowers on the counter, glancing at Eva before he addressed Jinx. She was used to making no impression on a guy like this. But that wouldn't last long,

"Chris is not." Jinx beckoned over another customer. Clearly he wasn't a fan.

The perfect man yanked an iPhone from his pocket and poked at it.

"Hi." Eva stepped forward, her hand out. "I'm Chris's sister, Eva."

"Uh-huh." He continued to peer at his phone, reading intently.

"The woman you're going to marry. We'll have beautiful children. I'm thinking five or six. We should get started on that soon, since I'm already twenty-eight."

He lifted his head suddenly. Their eyes locked. Well, hers locked. He kind of glanced at her, then did a double take, like, *What are you looking at?* "Sorry, what were you saying?"

"Nothing important." She smiled sweetly, held out her

hand again. *Just concerning the rest of our lives together. Or, more likely, the rest of the month.* "You were busy."

He made a sound of frustration. "Sometimes I'm not sure if I own the phone or it owns me."

"What's your name?" She'd bet this was—

"Ames Cooke."

Yup. The pain in Chris's lucky ass. The entitled, arrogant rich boy, who Chris had neglected to mention was devastatingly sexy.

Was he cocky businessman through and through? He certainly looked the part, but there was that gold stud glinting in one ear, and his slightly spiked hair. She was already thinking maybe a tattoo in a hidden place.

A place she couldn't wait to discover.

"You visiting?" Ames was looking around, undoubtedly still hoping Chris would emerge from the back of the shop.

"I'm taking over for Chris for a month."

His attention zoomed back to her. "Chris? What's wrong? Where is she?"

Look how nice of him to be concerned. A thoughtful guy. "She's at my place in California. We switched lives for a month."

"You switched—" Ames was clearly having trouble processing that one. But maybe the fact that his supposed beloved had left town without letting him know would help him understand that he and Chris were not destined to be together forever.

Whereas he and Eva…

At least for a month.

"Well, crap." He stared forlornly at the flowers, a stunning and almost laughably huge bouquet of pink roses, burgundy and white alstroemeria, white tulips, freesia and God knew what else.

"You could take them back to the shop. Or leave them here." Eva gestured around. "A little color and life wouldn't hurt."

"Oh." He stared as if he'd forgotten her. "Yeah, okay."

"Thank you." She took the vase into her arms as if she were cradling a baby and beamed at him. "So what are you doing tonight, Ames?"

As she expected, he looked startled, glanced at his watch, face reddening slightly. "I'm due at… I'm… I have…"

"Wow. That sounds fabulous."

He laughed in surprise.

"I just arrived today from California, so I'm going to take it easy tonight." She put the vase on the counter over the pastry. "Maybe order takeout, because I hear you can get anything delivered in this city."

"True."

She threw him a flirty look over her shoulder. "Even you?"

"Even me what?"

"If I was home bored and wanted company, could I order *you* for delivery?"

"I don't…" He took a step back. "That is…"

Eva waved dismissively and moved the vase farther down the counter. "Don't worry, I was only flirting. Cup of coffee on the house?"

"Uh." He laughed uncertainly. "Actually, I'm—"

"Jinx." She inclined her head toward the barista. "Give this man whatever he wants."

"Okay." Jinx stared coolly at Ames. "What'll it be?"

"Hmm?" Ames was lost in poking at his cell again. "Uh…a red eye. Room at the top. To go."

Eva took half a step closer to him. "We call those hammerheads in California."

"Really?"

"Really." She grinned at him. He was so adorable and so innocently unaware of the nights of hot sex that lay in store for him over the next month—and possibly forever. "And in the upper Midwest, where I grew up, it's called a depth charge."

"Okay."

Eva folded her arms across her chest. "So what do you do in this fabulous city, Ames?"

He muttered something, jabbing away at the little letters.

"Ames." Eva put her hand on his arm and pushed gently down.

"Huh?" He looked up at her. "I'm sorry. Did you say something?"

"I asked what you do in New York."

"I'm sales manager for Boyce Wines, a distributor based here in New York. We import from exclusive small family vineyards in Italy and France."

"Cool job. So you know a ton about wine."

"I guess." He shrugged and put his cell in his pocket, staring at her curiously. "Do you?"

"Just coffee." She took another step toward him, caught a whiff of his fresh masculine aftershave. "How did you get into that?"

"Dad owns a wine shop."

"Yeah? Where?"

"New Jersey." He edged toward the pickup area of the counter. "Are you this nosy with all your customers?"

"Nosy?" She sent him an odd look. "In California we call this conversation. They don't do that here?"

"Sorry." He had the grace to look embarrassed. "Been a tough day. So, California, huh?"

"Central Coast." She tipped her head, smiling alluringly. "Good wine country."

"Absolutely."

"Red eye. Room at the top." Jinx plunked the container on the counter.

"Sorry about your tough day." Eva folded her arms. "Want to talk about it?"

"I'm sure you have business to do." He reached for the cup.

"If I did, would I be offering to talk to you?"

"Ah." Ames rolled his eyes, smiling. "You *are* Chris's sister, after all. Or at least you have her sharp reflexes."

"Thank you." Eva frowned at the flowers, beautiful but oddly old-fashioned on the severe counter, as if the only flowers appropriate to the space would be square. "Have you ever meditated?"

"Uh. No. Listen, it was nice to—"

"It's great on a stressful day. You should totally try it."

"Mmm, not interested. Thanks."

"Doesn't hurt to try." She touched a spot on his forehead just above his brows, where Buddhists believed the third eye existed. He froze in horror, staring up at her finger, which made him sort of cross-eyed, but still incredibly sexy. Eva willed him to look at her, which he did, proving they had a deep connection. Or that he felt like looking at her just then. Their eyes held—both sets that time—and the adrenaline thrill was so strong she could barely get herself to continue. "It's amazing how calm and peaceful you can feel, while at the same time energized and clear. It's so different from how we usually operate, rushing around coping with external stuff and worries, ignoring our instincts."

He blinked. "Uh, yeah."

"And…" She lowered her voice, drew her finger down

the bridge of his very fine nose. "Meditating is also a very sensuous experience. You hear and see and feel and taste and touch the world in a whole new way when your mind is at peace."

The very delicious Ames swallowed audibly, then took a sudden step back, glancing at his watch. "Listen, thanks for the coffee. I really need to go."

"Sure, sure. You don't want to be late for your whatever." Somehow she kept her lips from twitching. "It was nice meeting you."

"Yeah. Same here." He turned and headed for the door.

"Ames!"

He turned reluctantly back, looking annoyed. "What?"

Eva pointed to the milk, sugar and stir station. "Room in your cup?"

"Oh. Right." He strode over and splashed milk into his coffee, jammed on a lid and rushed out of the shop.

She watched him go, hugging her hoodie around herself, a smile playing on her lips. What an amazing day this had turned out to be. She'd met her next true love, Ames Cooke, who didn't seem to realize they were meant to be.

The poor guy wasn't going to know what hit him.

2

CHRIS WALKED DOWN the hill from Eva's house, turned left onto La Playa Avenue and walked about fifty feet to Slow Pour. That was it! No trudging down windy cement sidewalks in the cold, with grit blowing into her eyes, no waiting for the subway in a pee-smelling tunnel, no swaying among sullen, silent strangers, then waiting in another tunnel for another train among more strangers...

In Carmia she could stroll to work in five minutes without a coat, and the smell was of ocean and earth. Not to mention Eva's store opened at seven instead of six, so she got to sleep nearly two hours later than in New York.

This was so fabulous!

Grinning like a fool, she navigated the assortment of colorful mismatched tables, which Eva had salvaged and painted herself. *Outdoor tables in October!*

Still smiling, she pushed into the shop. The place was adorable, homey, crowded, slightly shabby and very personal. On the sunny yellow walls were rainforest murals over which Eva had hung pictures of young Eva and Chris at coffee plantations throughout the world, and paintings by local artists that she sold from the shop. On an orange side counter were organic soaps, jewelry and cellophane bags of handmade chocolates, also the work of Carmia residents. Rotating stands held postcards and

Slow Pour tote bags, T-shirts and hats. Behind the main service counter Eva had mounted a blue surfboard on which she'd attached a whiteboard with the day's specialties scrawled across it in colored inks. Where the glass case at Chris's shop housed croissants, brioche, Japanese sweet buns, traditional English scones and Irish soda bread, Eva's held banana bread, carrot muffins, house-made granola bars and whole-grain pecan spice rolls.

Only one customer was inside, not surprising on such a beautiful day—a blond guy staring at the paper, which he abruptly put down when she walked in, and stared at her instead.

Rude.

She ignored him, walked to the counter, held out her hand to the petite blonde barista wearing an aqua tank top over the kind of light tan Chris was planning to acquire as soon as possible. This must be Summer. Her hair was wild and bleached by the sun, her eyes brown and friendly.

"Hey, there!" Her face broke into a warm smile, showing frighteningly white teeth. "Chris, am I right?"

"Yes, you are." She felt pale and drab in her charcoal shorts and beige cotton sweater. "Hi, Summer."

"I *knew* it." Summer looked so happy Chris felt slightly uncomfortable. "It is *so great* to meet you! Welcome to California!"

"It's great to be here. I'm just stopping by as a customer today, to say hello."

"I'm so glad you *did!*" She gestured to the surfboard menu. "Melinda is on the register this afternoon, but she had a doctor appointment. Can I get you something? I'll make it to go. You should totally go to the beach this afternoon."

"I was going to ask to look at the schedule and your sales data for—"

"Nah, go to the beach!" The guy at the table had the nerve to butt in. "You can look at sales stuff tomorrow."

Chris turned, incredulous at the interruption. "Uh, yeah, thanks."

"He's an every-day regular." Summer spoke under her breath, giving the guy a stunning smile.

"Gotcha," Chris murmured. She knew what that meant. No pissing off the good customer. She turned with a chilly smile. "I'm Chris. I'll be managing the—"

"Eva's sister."

"Yes." She had a sinking feeling this jerk was Zac, the guy Eva was planning to marry if nothing else worked out. Her sister's taste in men…well, it was pretty bad. Chris hadn't found Mr. Forever yet, either, but at least her relationships were counted in months and years, not days and weeks. And she never dived into one without looking or thinking, the way her sister always did.

"I'm Zac." He looked her over in a way that set her teeth on edge. "Wow. For a twin, you are nothing like Eva."

Was that a compliment or an insult? She didn't want him to think she cared either way. "I hear that a lot."

He stood and held out his hand, blue eyes crinkling in the corners, blond hair a few shades darker than Summer's. He was taller than she expected, and hot, in a California surfer-dude kind of way. Totally not her type. "I hear you're going to be around awhile."

"Just a month." She turned back to Summer. "I'll have a red eye, or whatever you call them here—coffee with a shot of espresso. And those reports? If you want, you can tell me where they are and I can get them."

"No, no, it's no problem at all." Summer stepped over to the espresso machine. "They're easy to find."

"You should get more sleep."

Chris stiffened, unable to believe Zac had just said that to her. "What?"

"Red eyes are caffeine on top of caffeine. If you treat your body well, it will give you all the energy you need on a lot fewer artificial stimulants."

"Yeah, okay, thanks, that's good to know." She groaned silently. This guy made Ames seem like a sweetheart. Too bad, because he looked like a more rugged version of Chris Hemsworth, aka Thor. But if he was a regular here, Chris would either have to learn how to handle him or tune him out—or have him abducted by aliens.

"Forget the sales reports." Zac put his hands on his hips, covered by worn jeans, which fit pretty fabulously, if you were prone to noticing stuff like that. Over them he wore a Dive and Surf T-shirt with a picture of a shark carrying a surfboard that had a huge bite taken out of it. "You should nap on the beach. You're probably jet-lagged and your body needs—"

"You know, I'm not really a nap-on-the-beach kind of girl." She balanced the acid in her tone with a smile as genuine as she could make it and stepped closer to the counter. "But thanks, really. I appreciate your concern."

"Sure." He didn't move. "Do you surf?"

"No!" She laughed. "Not a whole lot of that rolling in on Manhattan."

"You want to learn?"

"No. No, thanks." She tried to look politely regretful, but wanted to ask what he was smoking. Though this being mellow California, she might not want to know.

"I bet I can change your mind."

"Huh." She had to bite her cheek to keep from shouting at him. "Actually, it would be great if you didn't."

"I'll get those reports." Summer thumped Chris's red eye on the counter and disappeared into the back of the store, practically at a run.

"So you got sick of the big city, huh?"

Did he ever shut up? Chris turned back, arms folded. "What makes you think that?"

"Eva told me. I promised I'd help with your transition."

"Oh. Thanks, that is so nice." She wrinkled her nose. "But I'm an independent type. I'd rather find my own way around."

"Message received." He held up his hands, took a few steps back. "Not a problem."

Whew. He did have an off button. She breathed a sigh of relief. "Thanks anyway."

"Here you go." Summer handed the reports across the counter. "Everything should be there."

"Thanks, Summer." She left the store and stopped outside, face turned up to the sun, enjoying its warmth. Eva would have to fill her in on the best way to handle Zac. In the meantime, one of these tables out here was calling her name.

Ten seconds after she'd settled and opened the sales report, a Zac-shaped shadow fell over her table. "Chris. Do me a favor."

Her stomach sank. The guy was a serious pest. "What's that?"

"Follow me. If you don't like what I'm going to show you, you can come back here."

Her stomach twisted with irritation. "I'm fine. Really."

"Look here." He held his cell out in front of her nose. When she managed to focus, she saw a text. From her sister.

Zac is awesome. Go with him. Trust me.

"How did you—" Chris looked up in bewilderment, into his very blue eyes which were watching her with amusement, which made her want to growl again. "I thought you two had decided not to be in touch this month."

"This was an emergency."

Chris shut the report, praying for patience, and stood, radiating hostility she couldn't help. "Okay, show me. But so help me, if this spot isn't paradise on earth, I'll—"

"It is." He ambled across the sidewalk, not looking to see if she'd follow.

She did, but not willingly. In fact, during the walk she was wondering if there was anything she could put in his coffee that would keep him in bed for oh, say, exactly a month.

Down La Playa they moseyed toward the Pacific. Could he not move any faster? Chris had to shorten her steps so she didn't pass him, and her legs were shorter than his. What was he waiting for? Did he think she couldn't keep up? That she was some dainty flower? Forget that, she did triathlons every summer.

When she was just about ready to put a hand to his broad back and shove to make him go faster, they reached the end of the line of buildings and turned toward the beach.

Okay, okay, it was beautiful. Really beautiful. A peaceful expanse of sand flattened smooth by waves. On either side, rocky cliffs topped with sparse green growth and low trees. Zac led her on a short stroll across the sand, then up a steep path to the top of the cliff on the north side.

She followed him to a spot between two scrubby

bushes, where a table and bench had been set up so the occupants would be sheltered while still being able to take in the Pacific, the cliffs and the mountains behind.

"Wow." Chris put her hands on her hips, shaking her head in defeat. "You were right. It's perfect."

Zac shrugged his broad shoulders. "Seemed to me you can't improve on much when you're reading sales reports, but this might do it."

"It's beautiful. Thanks for showing me. I'll appreciate the quiet and privacy." She brightened her voice and put the report on the table with her coffee, praying he'd get the hint and leave her alone.

"Just you and the beautiful Central Coast." He lifted his hand for a high five. "Be at peace."

Chris slapped his palm. Whatever. He was going. "Thanks."

"See ya around."

She managed a noncommittal "Mmm." The second he was out of earshot, she furiously dialed her sister.

"Eva! What did you let me in for?"

"What do you mean?"

"This Zac person. He's horrible."

"*Zac?* Horrible?"

Chris rolled her eyes. She adored her sister, but sometimes she was much too…tolerant. Especially of guys. "He practically jumped down my throat. Told me I shouldn't drink red eyes, that I shouldn't read sales reports, shouldn't sit at the Slow Pour…"

"Oh, but isn't it gorgeous there where he took you? The cliff seat above Aura Beach, right? I told him he should."

Chris wrinkled her nose, gazing around her at the wide, endless ocean. "Well…yes, it's gorgeous."

"He wanted you to be happy."

"That's not the point. I was perfectly happy sitting outside at Slow Pour."

"Aren't you happier now?"

"No, I'm completely exasperated with him. And you!"

Eva giggled, making Chris smile. "He's a good guy, I promise."

"So what's he going to do, come in every day and tell me how to live my life?"

"Probably," Eva said cheerfully.

"Great." Chris rolled her eyes. "Out of Ames's frying pan and into Zac's fire."

"Ooh, into Zac's fire. Sounds like a sexy title. And speaking of sexy, you forgot to mention that Ames is a total hottie."

"Yeah…" Chris lifted her chin, letting the sun have at her face again. "He is kind of hot."

"Mmm." Eva sighed.

"Do not get any ideas. The guy's a narcissist. Not your type at all." It immediately occurred to her that Ames *was* Eva's type, since she invariably went for guys who were wrong for her. But that didn't mean she had to do it again.

"No? We'll see. Now sit down and enjoy the ocean for an hour or two."

"An hour or two? Staring at waves?" She snorted. "Not me. But it is a beautiful place to work."

"Chris, you just arrived! Enjoy the place!"

"I *am* enjoying it. It's stunning up here. Now leave me alone while I study your sales reports."

"You are hopeless."

"I know." She ended the call reminding her sister of a couple of restaurant suggestions in her neighborhood on Eighty-Seventh Street, and settled back with her report.

Hmm. Sales okay, fairly steady, but not really taking off. Looked a lot like her own track record in New

York, except most of Eva's traffic occurred midmorning and midafternoon, NYEspresso's dead times. In a place like—

"Whoa, sorry, man. Didn't realize someone was here."

Chris looked up, startled. She hadn't heard anyone com—

Oh, my God.

Dark windblown hair. Blue eyes. Shorts and T-shirt revealing a gorgeous body. Warm, white-toothed smile. The hottest guy she'd ever seen.

Her heart launched into triple time. She was unable to speak or return his smile, just sat there staring in a flood of hormones.

When was the last time a guy had affected her like this? Not John, not Rob, not even Steve, her most serious boyfriend. This crazy, overwhelming reaction was a first. What did it mean?

Something really good.

She took a deep breath and indicated the other half of the table. "Have a seat. There's plenty of room."

3

"Guy Chaumont Pinot Noir. Three cases? Four? Like last time. Okay, glad you enjoyed it." Ames scribbled on his notepad. "He's got an excellent Chardonnay, too. Twenty-ten, a classic dry Burgundy, with apple and melon notes, great with vegetarian and vegan dishes. Want me to bring a bottle when I see you Thursday? Okay, good. And the Chateau Moulin Bordeaux, too? Excellent. Nice talking with you and I'll see you Thursday at two. Right. Bye."

Ames tossed his pen onto the desk in the office he'd set up in one of his condo's extra bedrooms. Working from home was one of the greatest perks of his job and also one of its greatest challenges. Days like today, when he was restless and irritated, there was no one else around to bring him out of it except Jean, his Tuesdays-and-Thursdays cleaning woman, cook and sometimes assistant, who was convinced he couldn't live without her. She might be right. But her way of bringing him out of a funk was to tell him exactly how he was living his life wrong.

Didn't seem to help.

Finding out that Chris Meyer had left New York and flown about as far away over land as possible without telling him hurt more than Ames had expected. He'd been settling in for a slow and steady campaign to win her, and had thought he might be making some progress. To put it mildly, this didn't look good.

He pulled his laptop closer and brought up the file on Manhattan Vine, one of the biggest chains of liquor stores in the city, an account he'd singlehandedly landed for Boyce Wines, a coup that had been instrumental in getting him promoted in the venerable company. He'd spent the morning visiting retailers to check signage and point-of-purchase placement and probing managers for their openness to hosting wine-tasting events. He was thinking some of Manhattan Vine's east-side stores might be a good place to push Boyce's higher-priced wines now that the midlevel bottles had done pretty well.

Funny, the second he'd laid eyes on Chris he'd felt a pull, as if she was familiar somehow, as if he already knew her and it was only a matter of getting through the formalities of preliminary dates before they'd be together in a way Ames felt certain would be significant. He'd felt that way only once before about a woman and had ended up dating Sarah for four years before they came to a mutual realization that it was time to commit or break up, and they'd both chosen the latter.

In the intervening years, he'd dated casually here and there, but either he didn't fit her ideal or she didn't fit his. Until he saw Chris and felt so strongly that she had it all. Yes, she'd been reluctant, but he'd dealt with reluctance before and had overcome it with patience and low-key persistence.

This time...not so much.

Her crazy sister, though—man, that woman was... something else. Eva had looked at Ames as if he was her next meal. No, not quite that. More as if he was her favorite dessert. She'd made him uncomfortable, uneasy and also weirdly curious. Underneath all the look-at-me trappings she was attractive, and seemed spirited and funny. But definitely not his type the way her sister was. Beautiful, elegant, sophisticated, Chris was the kind of woman a guy could take anywhere and she'd fit right in, from a baseball game to one of the high-end restaurants and wine bars he frequented for business and pleasure. At the end of the month he'd hoped to take her to Boyce's annual dinner at La Grenouille Laide, one of New York's finest restaurants, and the company's most formal and important event, to which all their best clients and top sales people were invited. Delores, Mike Boyce's battle-ax secretary, had been on him to RSVP.

A reminder popped up on his laptop to call the Restless Armadillo restaurant, which hadn't placed an order in a while. He picked up his phone.

"I hope you're not staying home working again tonight." Jean, tiny and tough, about as New York as a person could get, never missed an opportunity to criticize everything possible about him. He adored her.

"How do you know I was home working last night?"

She tapped her temple. "I know."

"I *have* to work, Jean." He shook his head mournfully. "I have this really expensive assistant who all but drains my bank account every month."

"I'm playing the violin, boohoo. You're still young—what are you, thirty?"

"Thirty-three."

"Single and home at night. Sheesh." She threw up her hands. "I'm telling you, you're a catch. Even Manny says he'd date you. You should be out there finding someone to make you happy."

"Uh." He pretended distaste. "Your husband isn't really my type…"

"He's kidding, he's kidding. But *I'm* not." She put her

hands on her hips and glared at him, dark eyes enormous through her thick glasses. "Go out tonight. This stuff you're doing will keep. Your youth won't. You need to live."

"It's four o'clock. I need to get my work done so I can—"

The apartment phone rang, interrupting their latest standoff.

"I'll get it." She sent Ames a by now familiar look of disgust and stomped into the living room. "Hello?…Oh, hey, Frank….Uh-huh….Really?"

Ames stretched at his desk. Frank was the doorman. Probably letting them know about another change in the garbage pickup schedule.

"Sure, I'll hold." Jean appeared in the doorway of his office, phone held to her ear. "You expecting someone?"

"Nope."

"Maybe God answered my prayer and FedEx sent a nice single woman whose shift is just ending."

"Not expecting a package, either."

"You— *Yes,* Frank….Who?…Oh, I *see*….Is she pretty?…Young?…Uh-huh….Oh, she does?…Okay, sure, send her up."

"What was that?"

Jean ended the call triumphantly. "I got you a date."

"You *what?*"

"You heard me." Jean disappeared from sight into the living room.

"Who is it?" he called after her.

"Someone you know, don't worry. She's on her way up." Jean reappeared wearing her coat and a Yankees ball cap. "Anything you want me to do before I leave you to your wild night?"

"Yes." He stood behind his desk, hands on his hips, exasperated and a little curious. He couldn't think of any female friend who'd drop by during business hours without calling first. They all knew better. "Intercept whoever it is and tell her sorry, I'm busy, and to call first next time."

"Look at you all grumpy over a woman." Jean scowled at him. "You're a big boy, you tell her. I'm gone."

Ames rolled his eyes, more amused than annoyed. The visitor could be his college friend Kathy, back from a European tour. He'd lost track of her return date. Still, it would be strange of her not to call first.

The apartment doorbell rang. Jean's footsteps thudded over to get it.

"She's here already. The girl moves fast. I like her already." The front door opened. "Hello. I'm Jean Kajowski, Ames's hot live-in girlfriend. Just kidding. I keep house for him a couple days a week, though he doesn't like me calling it that. Don't worry, I was just leaving."

"Hi, Jean, nice to meet you." The voice was musical, sweet and vaguely familiar. "I'm Eva Meyer."

Ames sat back down abruptly. Eva was *here*? At his *condo*? *How* had she found his address?

"Hi, Eva. Oh, my God, your boots are adorable!" Jean was clearly smitten. "Come in, come in. He's in the office, probably shy. But he's not busy tonight, so don't let him tell you that he is. I'm off—bye you two."

Ames turned his eyes to the ceiling. Give him strength. "Bye, Jean, see you Thursday."

"Only if I live that long." The door closed behind her standard response.

Ames blinked at his office door. He could get up. But she'd stalked him here—she could come in on her own.

"Hi, Ames." Eva appeared at his doorway, smiling pleasantly, as if there was nothing strange about barging into his home when she'd met him for all of five minutes the day before. She wore a violently pink skirt under a bright green shirt and crazy floral sweater. Her chunky boots laced up to midcalf and were shiny fluorescent-green. She had about five earrings in each ear and an armful of jangling colored bracelets.

His eyes hurt just looking at her.

He stood. Picked up a pen. Put it down. She made him very uneasy. Staring at him with those bright blue eyes. He felt…he felt…

He didn't know what he felt. "What are you doing here?"

"I thought you might want to take me out tonight, since I'm new in the city." She lifted her eyebrows as if she had every right to expect an enthusiastic response.

"You—" Ames could barely take that in. "*What* made you think that? Don't you have to work?"

"My shift ended at two." She seemed totally comfortable in herself, not broadcasting any sense that her behavior was at all unusual. "I already stayed late for a couple of hours, catching up on things and getting to know more staff. Then I'd had enough. You can only take in so much new information, you know? So I came here."

"*Why?*"

She shrugged. "I don't know anyone else, really."

"Eva." Something was painfully misfiring under that bizarre hairstyle—randomly hiked up all over her head with multicolored combs that looked as if they were taking bites out of her scalp. "You don't know me, either."

"What better way to get started?" She smiled, looking around his office. Her mouth was generous, like her sister's, lips full, teeth slightly crooked. "Nice place. Totally fancy."

"Yeah, thanks." He should tell her to get lost now, before she got any more weird ideas.

"Here." She laid a NYEspresso bag on the table. "I brought you a cookie and a bag of espresso beans."

His eyes narrowed suspiciously. "How do you know I have an espresso machine?"

"Well…" She tilted her head to one side. A tattoo he hadn't noticed before rested at the base of her neck. She stood too far off for him to tell what it was. "Don't you?"

Ames cleared his throat. He had a reputation among his friends for being able to read women and communicate with them exceptionally well, both as friends and lovers. But with this woman he felt like a junior-high dork. "Yes. I do."

"Then you'll enjoy it. Very fresh, delivered this morning. Chris's special blend—Brazil with Ethiopia for some bite." She hoisted her hot-pink bag farther onto her shoulder and went to examine the books in his bookcase. "So where should we go? Chris and I have done the big tourist things, Empire State, Statue of Liberty, Times Square, Rockefeller Center, etc., but I would love to get to know some neighborhoods. Any favorites?"

He was out of his element here. Somehow she'd maneuvered him into feeling *he'd* be rude to ask her to leave. Yet he had every right to.

"You know, Eva, tonight might not be the best—"

"Jean said you weren't busy." She turned around holding Jamie Goode's *The Science of Wine*.

"Uh…"

"Oh, I see. You just don't want to go." She put the book back and approached his desk, mouth bunched slightly. "That's fine. I just thought it would be fun for both of us. Especially if you don't get out much."

"What makes you think I don't get out much?"

Again that head tilt. She was close enough now he

could see the tattoo was a tiny hummingbird. "Did you go out last night?"

"Not last night, but—"

"Night before?"

"No, not then, but—"

"Night before that?" She was enjoying this—her face was solemn, but her eyes were sparkling with fun.

He put his fists on his hips and glared at her.

Eva burst into laughter and shielded her face with her hands. "No, no, not the death-ray eyes. I was teasing you. Listen, I get that you're not interested. That's fine."

"Okay." He felt profound relief. And also...not. He dealt with it by picking up his pen again.

"By that I mean..." Her eyebrows lifted; the sparkle hadn't left her eyes. "That I'm fine going out with men who aren't interested."

This time he laughed. She might be a crazed stalker, but she was appealing in her own eccentric way, and obviously intelligent. "You're very determined."

"Hmm, how funny, Chris says the same about you."

He barely avoided blushing. "I guess she would."

"If you want my advice..."

"Not really."

Eva waggled her finger. "You need to give up on that. She's not going to change her mind."

Ames's jaw tightened. Disappointment and embarrassment that Eva and Chris had obviously been talking about what an annoyance he was.

He'd been so sure about Chris, had pictured her in his future, and it had felt natural and right.

Yeah, well, to hell with that.

"I'm sorry, Ames. I know you...cared for her in some way."

Her sympathy triggered an outraged testosterone rush.

He did *not* need pity. He was *not* a pathetic, lovelorn geek who failed in pursuit of women, *nor* was he a dork who stayed home every night working.

He threw his pen down. "I guess if we're going, we better get started."

"Oh, good!" Eva's face lit up. "I am in a totally adventurous mood. Where shall we go?"

"Greenwich Village." He answered immediately, hoping he hadn't just doomed himself to an exhausting and unbearable evening. But Greenwich Village was one of his favorite parts of New York, full of charm and the unexpected. Like Eva. She'd fit in fine there in her wild colors and crazy hair, because nobody didn't fit in there. And he was unlikely to bump into any important clients—or potential ones—who'd wonder why he was strolling around with a circus clown.

"I'm ready." She hoisted her pink bag, making her dozen or so bracelets slide and clatter.

He nodded and walked out from behind his desk, stopping to let her precede him to the door.

"Hey. Ames." She suddenly looked shy, tentative, very different from her usual brassy persona. Almost sweet. Her eyes were very blue, with dark lashes enhanced by mascara but not turned gunky, which seemed to be the style for too many women. Her eyebrows were natural, nicely arched. He could see the resemblance to Chris in the fine shape of her nose and the height of her cheekbones.

"Hey, what?"

"Thanks for doing this."

Something weird happened in his chest, a buzz of warmth that made him forgive her for interrupting his evening and making him feel like a loser—several times over. "Just don't make me regret it."

"Well, but…" She flung her arms out, let them drop in frustration. "That's half the fun!"

He couldn't help a grin. "I can still change my mind about going out."

"You won't." She preceded him out of his office. "You're not the type of man who ever goes back on a promise."

"Where do you get all these ideas about me?"

"I'm brilliant. By the way, this condo is *huge*. I swear your balcony is the size of Chris's entire apartment. You must sell a *ton* of wine."

"I do okay." Trust her to come right out and say it. Kind of refreshing, actually. "My parents bought the condo as an investment. When they retire, they'll want to move in."

"I'm not big on luxury. That's Chris's thing." She left his office, walking with surprising grace for someone wearing clump-around boots. "I'm an own-what-you-need kind of girl."

"Yeah?" He kept his voice neutral. He wasn't going to defend his choices to someone who wouldn't understand.

"But it's easy to be that way in the Central Coast." She turned to look at him, walking backward for a few steps. "I have mountains and ocean all around. In this city you'd need to create space wherever and however you can."

"True." He opened his front door to let her pass through, taken aback. She *totally* understood. As much as he loved New York, claustrophobia could be a problem. Unoccupied quiet space inspired an immediate *ahh* of relaxation, no matter where you found it. "After you."

"Thanks." She moved past him into the hallway, leaving a fresh, vaguely floral scent in her wake, not sweet, not overpowering.

A great smell, actually.

He locked the door and followed her to the elevator. He could have sped to catch up with her, but there was something mesmerizing about the nicely shaped sway of her pink skirt, the energetic strides of her slender legs in dark gray tights.

What was he thinking? This was crazy stalker Eva, sister of the lost woman of his dreams.

At ground level, Eva greeted Frank as if they were long-lost friends. Ames was astonished to see the generally somber doorman beam and blush, then nod at Ames, as if he approved of his taste in women.

No, no, no. Not this woman. Not *ever* this woman. Boyce Wines prided itself on its high-class, conservative image. He had clients to entertain; he wanted to be promoted to vice president of sales someday, maybe get into politics. He needed a woman who was— Who looked like— Who came across—

Ugh. Was he really that shallow?

No, not shallow, practical. He had to be honest about his goals and what he was looking for. Nothing wrong with that.

They walked along Forty-Third Street to Eighth Avenue and the Port Authority subway stop. The air was crisp and energizing—fall was Ames's favorite season. Maybe it was all those years of school, but to him September still felt like a fresh beginning.

The subway took them south to Fourteenth Street. They emerged back onto Eighth Avenue and walked farther south to Bleecker Street, where they turned to start their stroll through the Village.

The longer they walked, the more Ames had to admit he was enjoying himself. The weather was perfect, typical for October—cool but comfortable. Along the streets trees were turning colors and the buildings glowed with dark brick warmth in the fading light.

And Eva's eagerness was catching. Ames was something of a New York history geek, and this part of town had great stories to tell. He took her down Bedford Street to see a building Walt Disney had lived in, a detour to see the unexpected and peaceful private courtyard between two houses on Grove Street, then back on Bedford for a peek at number 86, a former Prohibition-era speakeasy and favorite hangout for writers that closed in 2007 when the facade crumbled into the street. Farther on, 75½, the narrowest house in New York, a mere nine feet wide.

By the time they strolled over to Washington Square Park, the sun was down, and Ames was getting hungry. Nothing surprising about that—he'd eaten a small lunch on the go several hours earlier. What *was* surprising was that he didn't want to ditch Eva and go home to eat. He wanted to keep their evening going.

"Feel like some dinner?"

"Love some." She put a hand to her flat stomach, causing an avalanche of bracelets to crash at her wrist. "I'm ravenous."

"You like Middle Eastern food?"

"Passionately!"

"Okay then." He liked that she answered with such… passion. He liked her enthusiasm for everything. It was easy in this town to become cynical, always in a hurry, to stop looking around and appreciating the small things. If nothing else came out of this bizarre forced date tonight, Eva had reminded him of that, and he was grateful.

He let the way to Mamoun's Falafel on MacDougal Street, a staggeringly popular place with minimal seating where he'd regularly stopped for late-night eats when he was a student at NYU. They bought falafel sandwiches with hummus and took them to eat on a bench in the park facing the small replica of Paris's Arc de Triomphe.

"Oh, m'gah." Eva spoke through a bite of falafel. "These are 'mazing!"

"Uh-huh." He couldn't think of another woman he knew who could talk with her mouth full and be somehow adorable.

"This whole *walk* has been so much fun."

"For me, too."

"Oh, good!" She turned and grinned at him. "So you'll ask me out again."

"What do you mean again?" He pretended to be mystified. "I didn't ask you out this time. You asked me."

"Hmm, yeah, good point." She looked perplexed for a second, then her expressive face cleared. "You can easily fix that by asking me out the first time and then again after that."

He snorted, getting used to her sense of humor. Enjoying it, in fact. "Thanks, I'll keep that in mind."

They finished their sandwiches, commenting on the scenery, discussing more of the Village streets she should explore on her next trip. A pair of NYU students passed them, backpacks on their shoulders, in earnest discussion. After them, a gay couple walking a terrier of some kind.

"The energy here is really different from farther uptown." Eva crumpled her sandwich paper.

"Yeah?" He refrained from rolling his eyes. The energy? This was New York, there was nothing but energy here. Who cared what kind it was?

"Funkier. Younger. More alternative. More like California."

He bristled, as any good New Yorker would. "Eva?"

"Mmm?" She was watching a black-clad teenage couple making out. He liked the way her hummingbird clung intimately to the smooth skin of her neck.

"Let me tell you something if you want to survive your time here. *Other* places are like New York. New York is *not* like other places. *Especially* California."

Eva turned to him, both eyebrows raised. He held her gaze, controlling any hint of a smile.

"Well, then. Only one thing to do." She leaned up and kissed him full on the mouth.

His body froze. Her lips were soft and lingered longer than a brief peck, but not much.

Then she sat back, took the last bite of her sandwich and crumpled the paper while he sat there like a dork loser with a half boner. "So what do you want to do now, Ames?"

He stared at her. Who kissed someone for the first time then acted as if it hadn't happened? How the heck did she keep catching him off balance like this? Just when he thought he'd reclaimed his terrain as Mr. Smooth?

What was he supposed to do now? Mention the kiss? Try to explain that he wasn't looking for any kind of relationship or romance right now (the phrase *with someone like you* didn't need to enter into it)? He'd look like a dork—again—making a big I'm-still-a-virgin deal over an innocent peck. Or not innocent. Didn't matter.

But if he ignored it, he'd lose an opportunity to set her straight. In the meantime she'd asked him a question.

"Uh. We could… There's…um… I don't know what…"

Oh, good one, Ames. He wasn't like this with women. *Ever.*

Eva sprang to her feet and held out her hand. "Let's find a place to have dessert. Or a beer. Or in your case, wine. How's that?"

He was surprised to find the idea appealing. "Okay, but on one condition."

"What's that?"

"No more kissing."

She looked astonished. "Why not?"

"Because…we're not the kissing… We aren't…" He broke off in utter frustration. "We're not supposed to be doing that."

Oh, God.

Dork!

"Ah." She put her hands to her hips and stared down at him as if he had four heads. "I see. You are morally outraged."

"*No,* no, I'm not.

"You didn't like kissing me?"

"*No,* that's not it. I mean…" He wanted to drop his head into his hands.

"Then…?"

Ames stood abruptly. "Let's get a drink. For God's sake."

"What a great idea. Wish I'd thought of it." She took his hand and swung it as they walked.

He was too grouchy to spar with her further. Her hand felt soft and warm and good in his. It had been a long time since he'd strolled holding hands with a woman. His last girlfriend, Taylor, had objected to walking that way, said it made her feel as though she was his daughter. That was strange, but whatever. Everyone had something that bugged them. Before Taylor he'd dated Patricia, who wouldn't go out on days she'd had her nails done. Before Patricia there'd been Ashley, who was so tender-hearted she couldn't handle movies with any violence. Nice women, all of them. Intelligent, beautiful, cultured, great company, but something had been missing every time. And then he'd seen Chris, and his instinct had kicked in so strongly.

"Are we going to walk to this place?" Eva asked.

Ames ended his reverie. No point thinking about something that was never going to happen. "We can or take a taxi. It's several blocks."

"Oh, walk, absolutely walk. I want to see everything."

"Fine by me." He had a new attitude about her boots. Too many women he dated wore heels so high they could barely make it to the end of a block without complaining.

"How long have you lived in the city?" She danced away from him, looking up, turned in a circle, then danced back, not taking his hand again.

"Since I was eighteen and came here to college at NYU from Jersey."

"Joisey, right. I'm from central Wisconsin, a town just north of Madison. Dad's a coffee scientist. Mom is an accountant. Does your mom work?"

"She helps Dad with the store. Bookkeeping, mostly." He turned up University Place, heading for Union Square, then Eighteenth Street and one of his brother's favorite bars, Old Town. There were a couple of fabulous wine bars in the area, customers of his, but he wasn't sure they could handle shiny lime-green boots.

Actually…this was New York. They could handle anything. The real question was whether Ames could handle them.

No, not really.

"Brothers? Sisters? Occupations?"

He sent her a look. "Are you going to keep this interrogation up all night?"

"Conversation, Ames, remember?"

"One brother. Mike. A schoolteacher."

"Ah, so you, the favored son, carried on the family tradition."

"I was always interested in wine. Worked at the store from age sixteen, read everything about it I could get my hands on."

"Drank everything you could get your hands on, too?"

"Tasted, then spat." He snorted. "If I drank every kind of wine I learned about, I'd be in serious trouble."

"How did you get started at Boyce Wines?"

"Dad used them for years at his store, insisted they were the best. He had a lot of respect for them and their business practices. So I applied, got a job, blah, blah, blah."

"Do you get to travel to vineyards? Hey, you can visit me in California!"

He wasn't going to touch that. "Boyce doesn't sell California wine. Just Italy and France."

"Then next time you go, I would be *happy* to come with you. Seriously."

He shot her a look. "Do I get to ask *you* questions now?"

"Wait. Wait." She dragged him out of the flow of pedestrians toward the street and pointed back at a building entrance they'd just passed. "Look at that!"

"What?" He saw a black awning with bowling pins on it. That couldn't be what had her so excited.

Please, no.

"Come on, let's check it out!" She grabbed his arm and pulled him toward the entrance. "I think there's bowling. This will be totally fun."

"Uh…" *Bowling?* "I'm not sure it's my thing."

"Of course it isn't. It's crazy. But how can you resist?"

If he knew how to answer that, he might be able to explain why he was still hanging out with her. Or how she got him inside the place and upstairs, where the place turned out to be some kind of amusement bar, decorated as homage to the preppy frat boy experience, with plaid upholstery, bowling, pool, darts and games of beer pong. Took him back more than ten years to his own college days.

Except he didn't want to go back there.

He bought two beers, hoping they could down them quickly and leave.

Of course not. In another room, Eva discovered a nine-hole mini-golf course, complete with models of animals— a giraffe, a gorilla, a zebra.... She was clearly thrilled.

Which meant Ames was clearly doomed. "You're going to make me play mini golf around large fake wild animals, aren't you?"

"Well, of course!" She hoisted her glass to clink with his. "Why waste such a golden opportunity to enjoy ourselves?"

Playing mini golf? There was no way he was going to enjoy himself doing that.

Over an hour later, he had to admit, he was enjoying himself. Yes, he would have liked a bag over his head in case he saw someone he knew, but there weren't any offered, and he didn't see anyone, so what the hell?

Plus, he'd learned two things about Eva. One, she was a killer mini-golf player. He barely squeaked out a win, pure luck, and when he jokingly accused her of throwing the game to save his ego, she insisted they play another nine holes.

On this round, he beat her at the giraffe. She got him at the zebra. He trounced her near the gorilla. She came back at him with everything and in spite of his pure-luck hole in one on the eighth hole, she beat him by two shots.

The other thing he learned about Eva was disturb-

ing. Maybe it was the beer—though they'd only had one
each. Maybe he was on the rebound from his disappointment over losing the hope of Chris. Maybe it was that the
evening had bounced him out of his usual routine, usual
company, usual destinations.

He was hot for her.

Her cheeks were flushed, her blue eyes snapped, her
bracelets jangled and she'd spent nearly the whole hour
laughing. At him, at herself, at the game, at the bar, at
the circumstances. A few locks of hair had escaped the
scalp-eating combs. Her sweater had all but slipped
off one shoulder, exposing smooth, tempting skin. She
moved with a very distinctive careless grace, and when
she looked at him, she conveyed an ancient woman-to-
man message he understood well.

He better go home and reestablish contact with all
things familiar before he did something stupid. Like kiss
her. Or more than that.

"Winner buys loser's next drink. I owe you." She took
his arm and propelled him, not to the bar as he expected,
but to return their putters, then out and downstairs to the
street, where the chill air and relative silence were refreshing after the crowds and noise.

"Now you can take me to the place we were going before I so rudely made you detour."

"Actually." He glanced at his watch, as if he had many
important things still to accomplish, when the only thing
he really had to accomplish was to avoid falling more
deeply under Eva's spell. "I should call it a night."

"Oh, okay, sure." She agreed so readily he felt a moment's disappointment. *Jeez, Ames, make up your mind.*

They headed one block west to Fifth Avenue, where
Ames hailed a cab. On their way up Avenue of the Amer-
icas, he kept the conversation impersonal, pointing out

Herald Square, Bryant Park and the back of New York's magnificent public library. His lecture ended when they turned onto Forty-Third and arrived at his building. Safe and sound.

"Here we are." He took out his wallet and extracted extra money to pay for Eva's trip home. Then he turned to smile and kiss her cheek in a platonic good-night.

He almost made it. But the feel of her skin under his lips, her flowery scent… Instead of jumping out of the cab and thanking her for a nice evening, he sat there, gazing at her.

Somehow she'd transformed from attractive to truly beautiful, her eyes large and glowing, her exquisite mouth curved in a smile.

Come on, Ames. Get the hell out while you still can.

"I had fun, Eva." He reached for the door handle. "Thanks for insisting I come out to— What are you *doing?*"

"Who, me?" She'd swung her crazily booted leg over both of his and had somehow managed to straddle him in the cab. "I'm just saying, 'You're welcome,' Ames."

"Jeez, you can't just—"

Yes, she could. She was already kissing him, hot, hungry kisses, pressing her pelvis against his.

He was a guy. That got a reaction. A fairly immediate and large one.

Wait, there'd been some reason he was going to avoid getting physical with her. It had seemed convincing at the time. Now he couldn't remember what it was. In fact, his hands were at her waist, traveling around and down to explore the pink skirt.

Oh, man. The pink skirt was firm and warm and fit his hands as though it was made to be in them. He wanted nothing more than to beg her to come up to his place so he could lose himself in what was under it.

But as suddenly as she'd climbed onto his lap, she climbed off, leaving him dazed and hard. Instinctively he moved to reach for her again, but a basic self-protective instinct kicked in and kept him still.

Thank God.

"Ames, I had *such* a nice time tonight, I really appreciate you taking me out."

"Hey, no problem, Eva. I had a good time, too. See you around maybe."

Only that wasn't what he said at all. What came out was more like "Ungh, yuh, too. 'Night."

Then he was on the street, still dazed, still half-erect, watching the cab speed away, a beautiful blonde beaming at him out of its back window.

4

EVA CHECKED HER WATCH. Again. Could this day go any slower? NYEspresso closed at six on Saturdays. They'd been fairly busy midmorning—opposite from weekdays, when the crowds showed up around the business commute—but since five it had been dead, and by now time had slowed nearly to stopping. Especially since the woman she'd scheduled to work the register, Rebecca, an MFA graduate student at nearby Hunter College, never stopped talking in spite of the fact that she had nothing to say. Eva had important things to do. Involving Ames.

It was tempting to close early, but Tom, a clockwork afternoon regular, was tapping away at his laptop as usual, earphones on, Mets hat on the table next to him, a frown of concentration on his face. He was one of those sexy geeks Eva always had a soft spot for. Another couple sat nearby holding hands across the table, each texting someone else.

Eva checked her watch again. It had barely moved.

Rebecca launched into a detailed new story about her latest project, featuring photographs of severed heads interspersed with painted images of cupcakes and hundreds of boxes of thumbtacks. Blessedly, Tom approached the counter, laptop packed up, and interrupted her. "Hey, Rebecca. Can I have a coffee to go?"

"Sure. Room at the top?"

"No." Eva answered for him. Rebecca needed to pay more attention to customers and less to herself. Tom always ordered the same thing. "Anything to go with that, Tom? Maybe a *pain au chocolat?*"

He hesitated, gazing at the burnished pastries under the counter. "We-e-e-ell. Okay."

"How did your work go today?" Eva let Rebecca ring him up while she got his coffee and pastry. "What are you working on? A novel?"

"Oh, no." He stood there sheepishly, unshaven, wearing his trademark black-framed glasses, shaggy head of dark curls, oversized Columbia sweatshirt, jeans and beat-up running shoes. "Nothing like that."

She waited for him to tell her, but apparently he didn't want to, so she changed the subject. "Do you live around here?"

"Nah. I live in New Jersey. In my parents' basement."

Eva reacted with a shocked look, then caught his sly grin and burst out laughing. "You bum. You almost got me."

He was even cuter when he was grinning.

"Sorry. It's a dumb joke. I live around the corner on Forty-Fourth."

"What do you do?" She was only more curious now.

"I'm a frustrated composer." His expression turned sheepish again. "Right now I'm working on a musical."

"How *cool!*" She let her mouth drop open in case he hadn't gotten how impressed she was. "Like for Broadway? What's it about?"

"It's a musical version of *The Importance of Being Earnest.*"

Wow! Still waters ran way deep. "I love that play!"

"Me, too. I'm—"

The door opened, and Natalie walked in, bringing with her a gust of fall-scented breeze. She looked stunning, as usual, her figure encased in skinny jeans tucked into brown suede ankle boots, a clingy sweater showing off her perfect figure. Around her neck was a neatly draped scarf, shimmers of gold glitter accenting the auburn highlights in her windblown hair.

Tom's mouth closed. Opened. He turned red. Took a step back from the counter as if he were trying to be invisible.

How *in*-teresting.

"Hey, Natalie." Eva gave her roommate a smile, which of course wasn't returned. Eva had learned not to take it personally. "You working today?"

"I'm always working." She came up to the counter, fumbling for her wallet. "I'll have a latte with soy milk. To go."

"Sure." Eva turned to the espresso machine, which she'd dubbed the Beast for its temperamental nature, and readied it to pull a double shot into a to-go cup.

Hmm…Natalie and Tom. Both into music and musicals. Natalie had stayed out late last night again, another date, Eva assumed, and had been up early. In Eva's opinion she was on a one-way track to health issues. A calm, solid sweetheart like Tom could be *just* what she needed—like a constant meditation session. The problem of course was how to get Natalie to notice him. According to Chris, all her men were as obviously gorgeous and fashionably put together as she was.

Eva finished steaming the milk, making sure it had fine, even froth, and poured it carefully into the cup of espresso, moving the pitcher back and forth to leave a flower pattern.

"Here you go." She handed over the cup and gestured

a few steps behind Natalie to Tom, who was staring worshipfully at the back of her head. "Natalie, have you met Tom Brewster?"

Natalie turned.

Tom flushed, stepped abruptly back and banged into a chair. "I've, um, seen you here before, yeah."

"Okay." Natalie studied him blankly while he fidgeted and she sipped her latte, coming up without a single bubble of foam on her lips.

Eva held her breath. *Come on, Natalie, say it, Oh, yes, I've noticed you, too, Tom.*

Nothing.

"I'm here all the time." Tom laughed awkwardly.

"Really." She did not sound impressed.

Eva jumped in. "Tom is a composer."

"No kidding." At least she was showing polite interest. "My dad teaches composition at Juilliard. Professor Adornetto."

"Wow. I took from him. I studied him. With him. I went to Juilliard. I guess you figured that out, though." Tom closed his eyes in a slow blink of misery. "Yeah, anyway, tell him hi."

"Sure." Natalie was watching him as if he had some kind of disability she might catch. "Tom Brewster, right?"

"That's it." He seemed pleased she'd remembered.

"Okay, well." Natalie glanced at her watch, her classic move just before the I'm-outta-here announcement. "I gotta get back to work. Nice to meet you, Tom."

"Same here. I'm sure I'll see you again."

"Yeah." She gave an icy smile and fashion-modeled her way out of the store, leaving Tom and Eva staring after her. Then at each other.

Tom sighed wistfully. "She's *so*…um, nice. She's nice. Seems nice."

Eva snorted. "Let's just say she needs the love of a good man, Tom. Keep trying."

"What? What do you—what?" He stepped back in alarm, bumping the chair again, blushing adorably. "I'm not—"

"Yes, you are. I think it's great."

"Nothing's going to happen." He gestured hopelessly. "I get so nervous around her, I can't even talk. She'd never look at me twice."

"Nonsense. You need to meditate and do positive visualization of yourself confident around her. Write down what you want to say to her and keep the paper with you." Eva smiled encouragingly, thinking how beautiful his brown eyes were, and how much she wanted him to be happy and also to leave now so she could close up and go attack Ames. "We're closing. You can go home and do all that now. Next time you see her, you'll be ready."

"If you say so." He spoke doubtfully, but thank goodness moved toward the door. "See ya, Eva. And thanks."

"You're welcome." Eva locked up after him and turned the sign from Open to Closed. She and Rebecca finished duties for the night, putting bakery items away and cleaning the machines. Finally Eva was able to shoo Rebecca out and rush into the back office to order Chinese food and get ready.

She'd taken a risk on Thursday by calling Ames's apartment in the afternoon, hoping Jean would answer. Happily, her prayers had been answered. Not only was Jean there, but Ames was out, and Jean was able to snoop in his calendar and had assured Eva in a voice dripping with exasperation that, yes, Ames would *again* be home on Saturday night—Saturday, for God's sake!—and wished her luck livening him up. Then she'd given Eva her cell number and told her to call any time she needed more help, because Ames was much too hot to be wasting himself at a desk every night.

Jean was awesome.

In the NYEspresso office, a tiny cluttered room barely containing the shop safe, file cabinet, computer desk and a chair, Eva darted to her gym bag—scarlet with a white poodle in pink-and-blue workout clothes on the side, which she hadn't been able to resist when she saw it online. She'd left her apartment that morning in a crushing hurry and had stuffed an armful of accessories inside it to experiment. Right now she had on black leggings and a black scoop-neck shirt—a blank canvas for the look she wanted to create for the evening.

Whatever that was.

She'd just selected an orange-and-yellow scarf when her cell rang. Chris!

"Hey, twin, how are you?"

"I'm sitting on that cliff overlooking the ocean reading a magazine. How do you think I am?"

"Oh, wow." Eva's heart gave a wistful throb. That was a fantastic spot. One of her favorites.

"Tell me what's been happening. Glad the shop is running fine—thanks for your texts—but I want to know how *you* are."

"Ah." Eva climbed onto a stool to see as much of herself as possible in the small mirror on the wall. "Guess who I had a date with last Tuesday?"

"Guess? Jeez, Eva, there aren't that many men in New York. This shouldn't take long."

Eva giggled. "Your personal florist. Ames."

"What?" Chris gasped. "You got stuck out with Ames? God, I'm sorry, Eva. What can I do to help you recover? Tea? A massage? Disinfectant?"

Eva's brows shot up. She stopped in the act of trying

to drape the scarf attractively around her neck—how did Natalie manage it? "What are you talking about? It was fabulous."

"You think sitting in a stuffy businessman's bar listening to him talk about himself is fabulous?"

"Uh." Eva wrinkled her nose and tossed the scarf onto her desk. Were they talking about the same guy? "That's not how it was. At all. We walked through Greenwich Village, he told me everything about its history, and then we ate take-out falafel on a bench in Washington Park and then we played mini golf."

Silence, except for incredulous noises from her twin. "Ames *Cooke?* Brown hair, brown eyes, gold earring, looks like—"

"Colin Farrell, yes! We had a blast. I'm totally in love with him. He doesn't know it yet but we're—"

"Oh, no. Not again, not with this guy. He is not your type at all!"

"What is my type?" Eva stepped down and rummaged through her gym bag, hauled out another scarf, teal this time, shot through with glittering red-and-yellow threads.

"You know, laid-back, kind of funky, New Agey, creative, a little out there. Like Zac."

"Uh-huh." Eva hopped back on the stool. "Have any of those relationships ever worked out for me?"

"Well, no but…well, no. They've all failed spectacularly. But that's because you dive in every time before you really—"

"So maybe that kind of man isn't my type after all!" She flung the scarf carelessly around her shoulders and turned back and forth in front of the tiny mirror.

Blech. No.

Off it came, thrown onto the growing discard pile. She wanted to look just right. Tonight she and Ames were going to have dinner at his place—she was buying—and then, oh, baby, they were going to get to *know* each other.

Only he didn't have a clue about any of that yet.

She'd given him several days to miss her terribly and wrestle with himself over what he felt and what he should do about her, while she got used to NYEspresso. Good strategy, but enough was enough. She missed him, missed his smiles and frowns and alternating exasperation and joy in their time together, and how hard he fought against letting himself relax and have fun. And how hard he fought the inevitability of their crazed passion.

"Did he tell you about that dinner?"

Eva extracted a glittering orange knit hat. "What dinner? When?"

"This big black-tie client dinner at one of the city's best restaurants. He asked me to go with him right before I left."

"Well, if he hasn't found another date yet, he can take me." She scowled at the orange hat.

"Are you kidding me? Stuffy in the extreme. You'd hate it. That's my point, Eva. I can't see you and Ames together. You're not his type, either."

"Yes, I am." She was back at the gym bag, pulling out a green brimmed cap. "I totally am. He just hasn't figured it out yet."

Silence, except for some by now familiar and increasingly loud noises of incredulity.

"Chris?" Eva paused, one leg up on the stool. "Do you need a Heimlich?"

"Eva…" Chris blew out a long breath. "You don't know the guy. You can't trust early infatuation. You should know that after all the relationship train wrecks you've had."

"Don't worry. It will take him a while to understand

that he feels the same way about me. I just have to make sure it's less than a month before he proposes."

"Before he—" Another sigh. "Eva, my darling sister, you sound like a crazy person."

Eva laughed and gave the hat a thumbs-up in the mirror, pulling her hair so it cascaded out of the material and over one shoulder. "Yes, I know. But I don't feel crazy, I feel fabulous. And if I get my heart smashed again, okay, at least I'll have fun trying, and someday I'll rise to try again. This is just how I roll. Now tell me what's going on in California. How's business? How are you settling in?"

"Well…now that you ask." Her sister's voice turned low and suggestive. "Zac—"

"Zac?" Eva nearly fell off the stool in her excitement. Chris and Zac? Why hadn't she thought of it before? How perfect! She'd found Ames, now Zac could fall in love with her sister, and vice versa. "You're dating him?"

"Who, *Zac?*" Chris sounded as if she'd just stepped in something disgusting.

"Oh. Guess not."

"God, no. He's so… I don't know, overbearing or something."

Eva rolled her eyes. Chris could be so judgmental. "No, he's not, he's a total sweetheart!"

Chris chuckled. "Wait, didn't we just have this same conversation about Ames?"

"Yes, yes. But then we shouldn't be surprised." She pawed through the gym bag, pulled out a green-and-white fringed poncho. "We figured out we have different tastes in men around age ten."

"You were Jesse McCartney, I was Daniel Radcliffe."

"*Beautiful Soul* vs. *Harry Potter*." She dropped the poncho over her head, careful of her phone. "So who'd you meet?"

"An incredible guy. Sweet, sensitive, sexy as hell. His name is Gus."

Eva's eyes shot open and stayed there. "Gus *Banyon?*"

"Yes! That's him! You know him?"

"Uh…yeah." She tried not to sound dismayed. Gus Banyon was a narcissistic moron child. "How many times have you gone out?"

"We just met once, then he had to go to some surf thing, but there's magic happening, I'll tell you."

Uh-oh. "Like bed magic or heart magic?"

"We'll start with one then see about the other. Unlike someone I know, I just think the guy's hot. I'm not planning to bear his children."

"Humph. I know what I'm doing." She hopped down from the stool again. Getting dressed in this tiny office was like a step aerobics class. From the gym bag, an outer pocket this time, she pulled out a pair of jade-and-silver earrings that looked like tiered fans and reached nearly to her shoulders. "But I also know Gus, and he's—"

"How well do you know him?"

"Well enough."

"About as well as I know Ames?"

"But… That's not… But…" Eva threw up her hands in surrender. "Okay, I get it. We both make our own mistakes and live with them."

"As if it's ever been any other way."

"I know, I know." She secured the second earring and lifted the phone from her shoulder, tipping her head the other way to ease the cramp in her neck. "So, I have finished making myself irresistible, I gotta go."

"Go where?"

"Not telling!"

"You're going out with Ames again, aren't you,"

"Maybe. What are you doing today?"

"Not telling!"

"Say hi to Gus."

"Say hi to Ames!"

Eva hung up the phone, giggling. Chris was a smart woman. She'd figure out sooner or later that Gus might be insanely hot, but he was also a member of a less evolved species. That was inevitable. In the meantime, Chris had some man fun to think about in her new surroundings, though why Zac had rubbed her the wrong way Eva couldn't imagine. If Eva could have fallen passionately in love with Zac sometime over the past three years since she'd opened Slow Pour and he'd become a regular, she would have. In fact, she wished she could call him right now, but he was crazy busy with applications and she was having adventures here, and they'd agreed before she left that it would be easier, especially if they met other people, to stay away from each other. Maybe he'd already fallen in love with Chris. Most guys did.

Having settled on her outfit, she left the shop and ran to Happy Family restaurant to pick up her order, then hurried around to Ames's building on Forty-Third Street, where she greeted the doorman, Frank, a friendly soul in an NFL player's body.

"Hi, Eva. I'm well, thanks. How are you this evening?"

"I'm in a great mood. Is Ames in? He's not expecting me." She held up the bag of takeout. "I've got his favorites."

She had no idea if Ames even liked chicken with black-bean sauce or shrimp with cashews, let alone loved them enough to label favorites, but she wanted in on Frank's good side.

"He's a lucky guy." Frank picked up the phone and dialed. "Hello, Mr. Cooke, this is Frank downstairs. Eva Meyer is here to see you."

She held up the bag and pointed insistently.

"With dinner," Frank added.

She gave him a thumbs-up.

"Ah." Frank's smile faded.

Eva faked a cough to cover her nervous giggle. Poor Frank. Poor Ames! All flustered and probably pissed off. He was perfectly welcome to tell her to go away if he wanted to.

She just hoped he wouldn't want to.

Frank hung up the phone and cleared his throat, avoiding her eyes. "You can go up. Six B."

Yes! She nearly keeled over with relief, already on her way to the elevator. "Thanks, Frank!"

Tick, tick, tick...the elevator could not have gone slower. At least she was alone, so no one would bear witness to her very entertaining dance of joy with takeout.

At the sixth floor, she tumbled out and raced for his door, then stopped and adopted a casual oh-so-cool attitude before she rang the bell.

Poor grouchy Ames was in for the night of his life.

5

Ames opened the door looking like a very sexy, disheveled, unshowered thundercloud. "Eva."

"Hello, Ames."

"What are you doing here?"

She held up the bag. "Bringing you dinner. What are you doing here?"

"I live here."

"So you say. May I come in?"

"Aw, jeez, Eva…" Ames shoved his hand through his bedhead, scowling. "It's not really a good time."

She gasped, pretending horror. "You have another woman over?"

"No." He spoke immediately and then looked as if he wished he could take the word back.

"You're in the middle of something really important?"

Ames glanced at the bag, then at her. The pungent, salty smell was enticing. "Uh…sort of."

"Work?"

He looked exasperated. "No, not really."

"Goofing off having a lazy, sloppy, smelly Saturday by yourself watching TV and planning cheese, crackers and beer for dinner and you don't want to admit it?"

He stared at her, then broke into a chuckle. "How do you *do* that?"

"Do what?" Eva blinked innocently. She hadn't *done* anything. She was just in good touch with her instincts. "Can I come in?"

"All right." He backed away from the door and gestured her in. "Welcome to my sloth."

Success! She walked in, trying to hide her delight, and looked around appraisingly. Shoes and socks on the floor, dirty dishes in the sink. "This isn't bad. You should have seen my room as a kid."

"You were a slob?"

"Unbelievable." She put the takeout bag on the granite kitchen counter and began unpacking cardboard containers. "Chris's room? She put everything away every night. I wallowed in mess. My mom would come in and yell, 'Until you pick this room up, I am *not vacuuming.*' Like that was a threat?"

"Ah, the rebel child."

"I'm guessing you weren't."

"Nah, that was my brother's job." He went to the refrigerator. "Want a beer?"

"Sure, thanks."

He put two bottles on the counter. Sierra Nevada pale ale. California beer. A good omen. "Are you still a slob?"

"Well…you can see some floor in my bedroom now. I need at least a few square feet to meditate every day." She folded the empty paper bag. "So have you been thinking about me as much as I've been thinking about you for the last four days?"

Ames got that frozen look on his face he did when she surprised him. "Uh…"

"Recycling?" She smiled blandly as if she hadn't just asked an incredibly personal question and held up the bag.

"There." He pointed to a blue can between the refrigerator and wall.

"I got the food spicy. Hope you don't mind." She turned from tossing the bag and held his gaze. "I really like it hot."

His eyes were amazing, large and dark and so expressive. Like now, it was obvious she'd freaked him out again. What fun.

Ames blew out a breath. "Um, I'd like to shower before we eat so I can feel human again. If that's okay with you."

"Sure, that's fine."

More than fine. It was perfect! Eva watched until he'd disappeared though a door into what must be his bedroom, then put the unopened beer back in the refrigerator. Crossing the living room, she waited until the shower started. Waited until the water had been running two minutes. Then she slipped into the large and attractively laid out but rather bland master bedroom, and headed for what must be the bathroom. Praying the door didn't squeak or creak loudly, she pushed it open a crack and peeked.

Ooh. Glass shower stall.

So nice.

This would work fine.

She pulled her head back, undressed down to what nature gave her, and tiptoed into the bathroom, where Ames was shampooing his hair, suds streaming down his face and chest.

Mmm.

So, *so* nice.

Ready or not, Ames, here you come.

"Hello."

"Eva!" His eyes shot open into the stream of suds. He jammed them shut immediately and swore. "What are you *doing?*"

"Joining you." She opened the glass door and stepped carefully into the shower.

"You are *not*—"

"Too late. Sorry."

Ames opened his eyes cautiously but didn't bother covering himself. Which, given that his earring was all he was wearing besides soap, and that he had a perfectly proportioned body in fabulous shape, was a wonderful thing.

Even more fun, while Eva enjoyed the view, Ames was giving her the same once-over, face to breasts, breasts to belly, belly to loins, loin to toes.

She didn't bother covering herself, either.

"Eva…"

"I thought you might like a little company." She glanced again at his really nicely shaped penis—not too big, not too small—which had already recovered from its shock and was rising to honor her occasion. "Apparently I thought right?"

He let his head drop into his hands.

Eva decided that would be a really good opportunity to see if his body felt as good pressed against hers as she imagined it would.

It did.

Ames groaned. "Why are you doing this to me?"

"Doing what?" She kissed his chin, kissed his chest, kissed one broad biceps, the other, then his chest again. "Making you feel wonderful? Letting you know I like you? And that I want you?"

She kissed one nipple, grazing it lightly with her teeth, heard him suck in a breath, which she took as permission to do the same on the other side. Then she thought it would be a really good idea to slide down his body to her knees and take his absolutely fabulous erection into her mouth.

His groan of pleasure told her she was right again.

"Eva."

"Mmm?"

"I should tell you to stop…"

"No, you shouldn't. Why would you?"

"Dunno." Ames sucked in a quick breath. "That…that feels very, very good."

She was glad. He tasted clean and male, slid smoothly in and out between her lips. She explored his balls, manipulating them, squeezing gently, feeling the textured skin tightening under her fingers as his arousal grew.

He widened his stance, put his hand to her head, stroking her hair, clearing it from her face, moving his body to redirect the shower spray when it hit her face and made it harder to breathe. Thoughtful. Almost tender.

She peeked up at him. His eyes were closed now, jaw jutted slightly, head tipped back, arm supporting him on the shower wall, stomach flat and muscled, pelvis moving back and forth, one of the sexiest sights she'd seen in a long, long time.

She increased her rhythm, fisted the base of his cock, swirling her tongue around its tip, reaching underneath with her other hand to stroke the hidden base of his penis.

Ames's eyes shot open, his lips parted.

Arousal jolted through Eva as if she was being pleasured herself. She felt extraordinarily in tune with him, not as if she were feeling her way with a new lover, but confident that she knew what would feel best to him, what he wanted, where, when, how fast and how hard. It almost seemed she'd become part of him.

This was supposed to be her seduction. Now he was seducing her, as well.

"Eva." His voice betrayed a touch of desperation, his breath coming faster. He was close; she knew it as if she was about to come herself, and renewed the pressure of her lips. Ames threaded his fingers into her hair, controlling her for one, two thrusts, then his hand tightened nearly painfully and he moaned and emptied into her mouth in bursts she let run out and mingle with the warm jets of water.

After another minute, the shower turned off. Silence except for Ames's slowing breaths.

Eva stood, not sure what to expect. Would he be angry at himself for losing control? For letting her continue? Would he be angry at her for intruding into his shower and seducing him into something he hadn't wanted to happen, except on an irresistible physical level?

He was so handsome, hair and skin glistening with water droplets, face flushed, eyes still darkened, grooves deepening around his sexy mouth. She was crazy about him. He was the one.

You know, probably. For a while, anyway.

"Whoa." Ames drew his hands down his face. "That was a surprise, Eva. Another one."

She stood still, arms at her sides, peeking up at him, still unsure of his mood. "A nice one?"

"A really nice one." He took her shoulders, watching her intently, as if he was trying to make up his mind about something. Maybe that's why she hadn't been able to peg his mood; he couldn't figure it out, either. "I guess I better get used to the unexpected around you."

Get used to it! That meant he wanted her around. That meant there would be more fun times. She'd done her job! They were off and running into the near future.

Oddly, she didn't feel the giddy rush of victory she expected. She felt rather solemn and slightly shaken. She was even trembling, strangely out of her element in a situation she'd instigated.

"I guess you better." Her voice was too high, a bit thin.

"You're cold." He opened the shower door and grabbed

a thick navy bath sheet, about the size of two of her towels. "Mind sharing?"

"Not at all." She forced herself to look perky and cheerful. "Looks like there's plenty to go around."

"Literally." He captured her in the thick, soft material, bringing her an inch from his face. She caught her breath, gazing into his eyes. "Hello, Eva."

Keep it light. Keep it fun. Keep it under control. "Why, hello, Ames. Fancy meeting you here in your shower! It's almost as if—"

He bent forward unexpectedly. His mouth was soft and warm; he kissed her lingeringly, leisurely, over and over, making her whole body tingle and her heartbeat all thumpy and strange.

When he finally drew back, she stared up as if he'd sucked out her brain, unable to think of a thing to say.

That had to be a first.

Her silence continued as he dried her with the king-size towel. Her back, her shoulders, her face and hair, gentle and thorough. Her breasts, her stomach, then he knelt to dry the backs of her legs, which meant his face was—

Ohh, my.

His tongue circled her clitoris, warm and slippery, pulled back, circled again, making her gasp. He knelt and parted her with his fingers, tasted the length of her, then settled in, licking and suckling her clitoris until her knees threatened to give way from the pleasure. She braced herself on the glass-and-tile walls of the shower and spread her legs farther, moaning when his finger slid boldly inside her, back, out and in again.

"Ames…"

"Mmm." He sped his rhythm, understanding her need without her having to articulate it—which was good, because she wasn't able to.

On and on he tasted her, patiently, persistently. Her orgasm teased, peered shyly around a figurative corner at some distance, then came closer, finally rushing at her in a hot charge that made her fall back against the wall as heat and ecstasy took away her awareness of anything but Ames's talented tongue and fingers.

She came down slowly, panting, her thighs trembling, her internal muscles still contracting sporadically, making her catch her breath with residual pleasure. "Oh, my goodness."

"You okay?" Ames stood, smiling smugly. As if he needed to ask?

"I am forever altered…" She smiled shyly back, wondering if it would prove as true as it felt, though of course he'd take it as more of her nonsense. "For one thing, I'm not sure I'll ever walk again."

"Uh-oh. You better let me help you." He pried her off the wall and escorted her gallantly out of the shower as her legs gradually steadied, his cock half-hard in reaction to her orgasm. *Very* hot when men enjoyed oral sex that much.

"On second thought, I'm miraculously unharmed." She retrieved the towel and wrapped it around his broad shoulders, pulling him to her for a brief peck, wanting more of those deep, lingering kisses, but afraid to get that intense again so soon. Maybe she wouldn't even bring up wedding plans until their next date, ha-ha. Certainly for the rest of tonight she'd stay away from anything more complicated than pure fun. "But I am starving."

"I happen to have a slightly cooled Chinese meal for two ready and waiting." He dragged the towel across his arms and started on his legs.

"What an amazing coincidence." She grabbed her

panties and stepped into them. "Let's turn up the heat and eat in our underwear. Pretend it's a beach picnic."

Ames blinked at her. She loved when he got that flustered look on his face, like, *What the hell is this woman's problem?* Then he always seemed to come around.

"Okay. But…Eva…"

"Yes…Ames…?"

He grinned briefly, pulling on navy boxer briefs. "At some point we need to talk about what happened here."

"Oh, yes, we should do that right now." She hooked her bra behind her, nodding earnestly. "See, you were in the shower, and I decided to join you, so I stepped in, got on my knees and took your beautiful erect—"

"Uh—not quite like that." He led her out of the bathroom into the cooler air of his condo.

"We can talk on the beach while we're eating."

They should talk, absolutely. Eva would say, "As far as I'm concerned, this is just for fun," and Ames would say, "That's what I was thinking, too," and then they'd agree to have a wild fling for the next three weeks, during which one or both of them would fall madly in love. Certainly Eva was well on her way already. At the end of three weeks their tryst would end beautifully and tragically because she'd have to go home to wait for Zac or her next affair, whichever came first.

She wasn't sure if all that sounded as satisfying as it usually did.

While she got spoons, forks and plates for the food—and sneaked a couple of condoms from her purse into the bag with the fortune cookies, because the night was young and so were they—Ames cranked up the heat and took the beer out of the refrigerator again.

"We can eat in here." He led the way into the living

room. "No palm trees, but the beige carpet makes for good sand."

"Perfect sand." Eva followed him into the elegantly furnished room, done mostly in earth shades—olive couch, brown-and-ocher chairs, dark brick around the fireplace. It looked like a showroom, as though no one really lived here. Kind of like NYEspresso. Beautiful but cold.

"I have another idea." Ames grabbed a remote and logged in to the internet to display on his flat-panel TV. "I bet we can find videos of beach waves on YouTube."

While he searched, Eva looked around the room, imagining plants and posters, colorful rugs, art books... "Ames, I've decided your place needs something."

He shot her a glance. "I'm afraid to ask."

"No, no, nothing weird." She pointed to a corner. "Right there. A gorilla statue and a hole of mini golf."

"Um, yeah, I'll get right on that." He backed away from the set, watching expectantly. A video started, waves crashing onto a glorious sand beach, palm fronds fluttering in the wind.

"Oh, Ames." She came up next to him and hung on to his shoulder, watching. "How sweet of you to bring me all the way to Maui when you barely know me!"

"I'm that kind of guy." He puffed himself up, looking magnificent instead of comical as he intended, chest sexily sprinkled with hair, legs solid, and one hot pair of royal-blue boxer briefs generously outlining his very nice package.

"You know—" Eva helped him push the couch back so they'd have plenty of "sand" for their beach picnic, and spread out a bedspread he retrieved from a closet for the food and plates "—I've been thinking about NYEspresso. It needs something, too."

"Gorilla mini golf?"

"Not necessarily. Though that's always a good look." She knelt beside him and helped herself to a plate of fragrant food and a good mound of rice. "I spent yesterday touring other indie coffee shops in about a five-block radius. There are so many like NYEspresso, you know? Chic, elegant. I feel like it needs a little…loosening. A shot of California, maybe. I'd like to see what would happen if I added some fun, gave people a break from the New Yorkness of New York."

Ames shook his head pityingly. "Only people from California think New Yorkers need a break from New York."

"I'm betting they do." She shook her fork threateningly at him, wanting to put down her plate and straddle his fabulous muscular thighs, but the food was too good to put off any longer.

"So what are you thinking of doing?"

"Not sure yet." She traded her plate for a sip of beer. "Obviously nothing that would be a permanent change and nothing Chris would hate. But I thought a little experiment wouldn't be terrible."

"Like…"

She waved her beer through the air. "More color. Plants, even fake ones. Something to soften the sharp edges, make people feel like they're walking into a different world, if not a tropical zone then at least a temperate one. Especially now, when fall is reminding everyone that winter's coming."

"Hey, I know! How about one of those thunderstorm soundtracks? Every thirty seconds it can sprinkle rain on everyone!"

"So, I'm curious." Eva gazed at him, thoughtfully

deadpan. "How did you ever get to be respected in the business community?"

He cracked up. "Because I'm so damn charming."

"You are." She let her face relax into a smile. "At least I think so."

"Yeah?" He put down his plate, set his beer on the coffee table behind him. "So…what are we doing here, Eva?"

"We're eat—"

"*Don't* say we're eating Chinese food."

"Ugh. I'm predictable already." Eva set down her plate, too, still clutching her beer so it wouldn't tip, though it also felt comforting to have something in her hands. "I think the question is not what are we doing, but what do we *want* to be doing?"

"Fair enough." He grinned, lacing his fingers behind his head. "You first."

"Oh, thanks." She rolled her eyes, stalling her answer with a swig of beer. Nothing too emotional, nothing involving the word *relationship* unless it was clear she was kidding. "Okay. What I want to be doing is…you."

"Ah."

"I'm leaving in a month. More like three weeks now. I don't think we can make it to the altar by that time, so I'm happy just taking some time to enjoy each other." She managed a careless shrug, shocked at how tough it was to talk about this with him. "If that's what you want, too."

"I'm…" He put his fork down, stared at his plate. "I guess I was thinking more just tonight, Eva."

"Oh." She contained her disappointment. She counted on the next three weeks to make this man fall head over heels in love with her, which he'd already started to do even if he didn't know it yet. "Well, okay."

"I'm sorry, I just…don't want to get in any d—"

Eva's hopes rose. Deeper? Maybe he had started to recognize his feelings for her. Not a great sign that he was fighting them, but she wouldn't have to consider this a final defeat. "I understand, Ames. Truly. We're consenting adults. Pouncing on you in your shower doesn't mean you owe me more than what I asked for, which was exactly that. Tonight."

She waited, fingers figuratively crossed. If he looked at all disappointed she had a chance.

His face was priceless. At first surprised, a touch of relief, but then, *ooh,* the way he stared pensively and slightly crankily at his food—was that male ego a bit dented by her easy acceptance of his limits?

She hoped so. Even if tonight was all they had, at least he wasn't throwing her off without another thought.

She got up on her knees and waddled over to him, put her beer on the table alongside his. "So tell me, Ames."

"Huh?" He looked as if she'd interrupted some pretty deep soul-searching.

Excellent.

"Does our one-night stand include the rest of tonight, or is what we accomplished already in the shower the extent of our shared physical activity?" She put her hands on her hips, fluttered her eyelashes sweetly, pretending his answer didn't concern her one way or another, though she was pretty sure she knew what it would be.

"Hmm." He got to his knees, too, finger comically tapping on his chin. "Let me think about that for a while— okay, I'm done."

He pounced, rolling her back onto the bedspread covering the floor.

"Ames!" She squealed in a delighted protest. "You're lying on my Chinese food."

"You're lying on my sand. It will get all up in your bikini."

"You know, you're right." She frowned down at her body. "I think I should take it off, don't you?"

"Please let me help you."

"You are *so* thoughtful." She looped her arms around his neck and lifted her hips so he could slide off her panties.

Even though he'd already seen her naked, the way he studied her emerging skin and female parts as if he were unwrapping the most remarkable gift he'd ever gotten— well, a girl could get used to that type of reverence. She sure would like to.

Keep it light... "Everything still there?"

"Everything is perfect." He ran his hand over her stomach, down between her legs, a light caress that made her shiver.

"Except one thing." She stared pointedly at the appetizing bulge in his boxer briefs. "You are still wearing your suit."

"You're right, I am." He rolled onto his side, frowning. "Any idea what to do? I've got nothing."

"Doesn't look that way to me." She reached for his waistband. "However, if you cooperate, I think I can help you."

"Thanks, Eva." His smile faded as her fingers slid under and closed around his erection; his breath caught. "Oh, man. I love the way you touch me."

She loved making him feel good like this. His face was so dear to her already, she could scarcely believe how briefly they'd known each other. But that was how she rolled, not dipping her toe in to test waters, not stepping in gradually to adjust to the stream, but throwing herself in, body and soul. If that meant she got hurt more than most people, okay, she'd take it. But she'd never be accused of hiding from life and all it could offer.

"On your knees, boy," she whispered.

"Yes, ma'am."

She rested her breasts against his warm, hard chest, rubbed them back and forth, enjoying the stimulation as she eased his boxer briefs down, circling his tight, beautiful buttocks lightly with her fingers. "Off with the underwear."

He obeyed. She watched him, enjoying the play of his thigh muscles, the careless way he flung the briefs aside and came back to her.

"Fortune cookie?" She grabbed up the bag and offered it, trying to look nonchalant.

"What, *now?*"

"When better?"

He shrugged, reached in and held up a condom in disbelief. "*What* restaurant did you order from?"

Eva giggled. "Best in town. Full service."

"Apparently." He put the packet on the ground next to them. "I have some we could have used, Eva, but thanks for coming tonight all prepared for my coming tonight."

"I look forward to your coming tonight." Still on her knees, she swayed forward until their bodies were touching again. "And you're welcome."

His eyes darkened, his arms closed around her. "You'll be coming tonight, too. That okay with you?"

"Oh, yes."

"Good." He kissed her leisurely, his fingers roaming around her back and down to circle her bottom, then up, around, down, up again…. His hands were warm, possessive, and felt so wonderful on her body she wanted to purr.

"Nice," he murmured. "You feel very nice."

"You, too." She leaned back to draw her hands across his chest, loving the smooth dip and swell of his pectorals, the round muscles of his shoulders, the smooth sweep of his back.

His fingers made an oval up and around her hip bones, then descended toward her sex, stroking and exploring while he kissed her.

He had the most perfect way of touching her, delicately at first, then a firmer tease, then backing off again. Her desire rose, waned, rose, waned, two steps forward, one back, three forward, one back, four, five, then she was way hot wanting him.

"Ames," she whispered. "I'm so ready, I'm about to scream."

"I like that about you." He picked up the condom.

Eva knew exactly how things should go from there. Not intimately, not face-to-face, where the emotion would have an opportunity to grow. If she wanted more nights with him, she'd have to play Scheherazade and leave him wanting more, not less. Sex would be its own reward, erotic and fun.

She lowered herself to her side and slid her bottom leg between his, raised her upper leg and wrapped it around his waist. "Ever tried this?"

"I'm about to." Ames grabbed the leg folded around him to give her support, and pushed gently inside her, both of them moaning in pleasure at the penetration.

"Mmm." He felt fabulous, full and long, filling and stretching her, going deep and deeper still. Eva loved the angle, loved the feel of his thigh muscles working as he pushed in and out.

She drew her hands up her stomach, over her breasts, stroking them, rolling her nipples between her fingers.

His breath hissed in. He slowed his pace. "If you keep doing that I'm going to come before you do."

"Is that so terrible?" She smiled up at him.

"Ladies first."

"Hmm. You know, I don't really feel like a proper lady right now." She slid her hand down between her legs, circling with a finger, loving the double stimulation of the cock inside her and the direct touch on her clit.

"Eva." He gripped her knee hard, pushing desperately. She held his hot gaze as she touched herself, the warmth growing, her orgasm approaching.

"Ames." She pushed back against him, rubbing harder, her breath hitching. "I'm going to come."

His face contorted, his movements grew jerky, spasmodic. He thrust hard, backed off, thrust again.

Eva closed her eyes and cried out as the climax swept her, heard Ames groaning, then felt his release pulsing between her legs.

So beautiful. So wonderful. So perfect between them.

If after this, tonight was still the only night Ames wanted with her, then he wasn't the man for her after all.

But she had a feeling she'd just bought herself a pretty fabulous three weeks, to do all this again and maybe a whole lot more.

6

CHRIS STOOD IN her sister's bedroom, windows wide open—wide open in mid-October!—catching the soft flow of a Pacific breeze. She was getting ready for her date tonight with Gus, back home after his…surfer thing. He hadn't exactly called it a date, just asked if she wanted to "hang out," but the chemistry between them was so blazing and out of control, he couldn't have meant anything else.

She was giddy—she couldn't help it. This kind of crazy lust at first sight was what Eva did, not her. Sensible, cautious Chris always carefully weighed pros and cons before she moved forward. Hired to work the register at Fine Grind, she'd moved up, learning the business until the owners made noises about selling and she'd stepped in. Even then, there had been meetings, business plans and a thorough investigation of the pros and cons. Eva, looking for a house on the Central Coast, had stumbled over a run-down tourist shop near bankruptcy and snatched it up. Untried location, entirely new business. Chris never had sex on the first date, never gave in to impulse buys and always refused the second piece of cake. When she was little, for fan clubs and birthday parties, she'd draw up extensive plans and organizational charts. Eva lived most of her life on impulse.

The strange thing? Both approaches had brought the twin sisters to pretty much the same place. Both were owners of shops that were doing well but could do better. Both had survived a string of relationships that hadn't worked out—Chris's started slower and lasted longer, but the end result was the same.

So maybe the method didn't matter in the big picture of success.

Or maybe she was trying hard to justify wanting to jump Gus's bones before he even opened his mouth tonight.

The day had taken forever. Few customers had come in. She'd had a lot of time to think about Slow Pour. The location was great, but…she wondered about the store itself, which seemed so much like other shops in the area. She couldn't help thinking about trying a few changes. Decluttering the space, focusing on fewer items for sale. Trading some of the laid-back central California vibe for a more trendy-chic energy. Maybe people would respond to something a little different?

Chris would check with Eva before she made any changes, of course, though she wouldn't do that until her ideas had coalesced and she had a more concrete idea of what changes to suggest. She'd call Eva soon anyway to find out how her plans to catch Ames—*Ames,* of all people!—were going. But not right now, even though a chat would kill off the last fifteen minutes until Gus picked her up. She didn't want to hear from her sister what a loser Gus was. Not right before she'd be seeing him.

A frisson of excitement went through her. She flopped onto Eva's bed, landing in the middle of her assortment of fish-shaped pillows. Where would Gus take her tonight? A romantic restaurant for an intimate dinner? Then out dancing? Finishing with a drink by candlelight and a stunning view of the ocean? Then maybe…back here? His place? Only if it felt right.

Giggling, she flung herself up to sitting, then bounced off the bed, smoothing her top. She'd worked hard to pick an outfit that would fit in anywhere. Royal-blue linen shorts and a close-fitting sleeveless white tunic that hit her figure in all the right places without being obvious. Simple jewelry—earrings with lapis lazuli stones to match her shorts, necklace a glittering zigzag snake with blue eyes and a thin bracelet in plain gold. On her feet, heeled blue sandals with straps crisscrossing up her ankle.

On the radio, one of her favorite Fall Out Boy songs blared, "This Ain't a Scene, It's an Arms Race."

She looked great, she felt great. This would be a good night. And if going crazy didn't appeal, nothing said she had to. But she was ready. Too many nights spent here being mellow, taking walks, exercising…. She was used to having too many choices of activity, not too few.

Her doorbell rang. She grabbed a tiny white purse and slung its gold chain strap over her shoulder, hurrying to the front door, where she took a moment to make sure she looked relaxed and as if she went out with incredible hunks every night.

Sure she did.

Okay, go. She opened the door, big smile in place.

God, he was hot! Tousled dark hair, sun-kissed skin, strong stubbled jaw, piercing blue eyes.

In the next microsecond, she registered that he was wearing baggy camouflage shorts, a worn T-shirt and old flip-flops.

Oh, crap! Chris was ludicrously and prissily over-dressed.

"Hey, Chris." He looked her up and down. "Whoa. You look amazing."

"Thanks." She held her head up. Not going to apologize. He hadn't told her to dress casually. Though maybe "hang out" should have tipped her off. "You are very handsome yourself."

"Yeah?" He seemed unsurprised by the compliment. "So, I thought we could go hang out at this sweet surf spot. I am really digging the waves today."

"Oh." Her face fell. Strike two. "But I don't surf."

"No problem." He grinned, his teeth white and even. "I can surf enough for both of us."

Uh... Chris stared at him, smile frozen on her face. He wanted her to sit on the beach and watch him surf?

No, no, he couldn't mean the whole afternoon. Maybe a couple of runs, she'd tell him how great he was, then they'd hang out on the beach and talk, maybe get some dinner later on. Not what she expected, but that was fine. He was clearly anxious to impress her. Guys weren't always subtle about that. "Why don't I change into something more beachy?"

"That would be good. I'll wait." He strode into Eva's kitchen and opened the battered stainless refrigerator, which Chris had spent an hour cleaning her first day here. "Got any organic juice?"

"Uh. Tropicana?"

"Dude, you gotta try Suja Juice. It's awesome."

"Really." *Did he just call her* dude?

"Yeah, it's cold pressed from organic fruit. No vitamins destroyed in heat processing. They call it 'epically refreshing.'"

"Epically." She nodded several times. The word *epic* made her think of *Gone with the Wind* or *Lord of the Rings* or *The Iliad.* Not so much juice. "Well, I'll have to try those. Be right back."

"Sure." He was still inspecting her refrigerator. She

hoped he didn't notice her half-finished bottle of Yoo-hoo. Or find the cheddar cracker and peanut butter sandwiches in the cabinet. Good bet neither of those was organic.

In her bedroom, she replaced her pretty outfit with tiny denim shorts and a cropped blue-and-white top, leaving on the jewelry. The blue sandals she replaced with waterproof Tevas Eva had left behind. While Gus was surfing she could walk at the water's edge, dip her toes in. That would actually be great. She'd been so busy at Slow Pour and touring nearby competitors, she hadn't spent as many daylight hours at the beach as she'd wanted. And it wasn't as if Gus was planning to surf for hours.

He surfed for hours.

Or at least it felt that way. Chris loved it at first, watching him paddle out to the spot he deemed best, his strong shoulders and arms propelling the board. She'd waited for him to start riding wave after wave in spectacular fashion.

Unfortunately, she figured out really quickly that surfing was about as exciting to watch as golf. For every wave Gus went for, there were about a hundred he let pass. Watching someone bob up and down sitting on a board was just not that absorbing.

She explored the beach for a while, walked along the water's edge for a while doing the toe-dip thing, lay in the sun for a while, watched some kids playing in the sand with their mom for a while, and then…

Just sat there.

Every now and then Gus would wave cheerfully from his stupid bobbing board. Or he'd cup his hands over his mouth and yell something she couldn't hear and she'd have to shrug and shake her head in pantomime. After the first few runs, she'd cheered enthusiastically, expecting each time that he'd come the rest of the way in, sit next to her and make plans for their next stop.

Yeah, that didn't happen. Gus would end his run or fall, then he'd paddle right back out. And he'd sit there. And sit there. And sit there.

Chris was very tempted to get up and leave, but they'd driven in his car to an unfamiliar beach and she had no idea where she was or how to get home.

To put it mildly, her lust was cooling. She'd been so primed to spend the evening in a thrilling haze of something-could-happen. Or even better, in the throes of something-is-happening. She'd been stoked and ready to be unsensible and uncautious and to do whatever she felt like.

"Hey! *Chris.*"

Chris turned at the familiar voice, sick dread in her stomach. Oh, no. Not him. *Zac.* As if she needed another gorgeous and disappointing man around tonight. She was almost homesick for a typical speed-through date with a neurotic and entitled New Yorker.

Almost.

"So." Zac dropped onto the sand beside her as if they'd planned to spend the evening together and he was about to apologize for being late. "What's going on?"

"I'm here with a friend." She gestured out at the bobbing Gus dude.

"Yeah?" Zac shaded his eyes to peer out. "Who's that?"

"Gus Banyon."

"Gus, huh." He stared at her curiously. "Something going on there?"

Yes, I'm carrying his octuplets. "Is that really your business?"

"Nope." He shrugged, dug up a handful of sand and let it slide through his fingers. "Just wondering. He doesn't seem your type."

"Ah." She wasn't going to ask what he thought her

type was. She wasn't going to ask him anything. Maybe then he'd go away.

Though she had to admit he was not tough to look at. If he'd shut up, she wouldn't mind having him around all that much. At least he was here beside her instead of out in the waves playing shark bait.

"How long has Gus been out there?"

Forever. "Oh, gee, I'm not sure. A while."

Zac snorted. "If I know Gus, he won't come in until it's dark."

"Oh." Chris kept her features bland, fuming inside. Until *dark?* What was *wrong* with the guy?

"Gus really loves to surf. He's on track to go pro, did you know that?"

"No." Chris wasn't going to admit that she didn't even know people surfed professionally. Like, really? You could get *paid* for sitting there bobbing up and down?

"But I think he kind of forgets that other people don't love it the same way."

"I see." She was really pissed off now. One date had tanked and now she was apparently stuck with another one she never wanted in the first place. "Doesn't anyone have normal office jobs around here?"

"Nah." He grinned at her.

His smile made it hard to stay properly pissed off, which pissed her off even more. "I didn't think so."

"How's it going at Slow Pour?"

"You're there every day." Oops. She hadn't meant to sound that bitchy. "How do you think it's going?"

"Seems fine to me." He lay back on his elbows, stretched his long, muscular legs out in front of him. He was a big guy, lean and lumbering, not like Gus, who sizzled with slender sexual energy. "But I want to know what you think."

"I like it there." She tried to sound gentler. It wasn't Zac's fault her evening had started rough.

"I saw pictures of NYEspresso online. Totally different concept, huh."

"Different cities. Different sisters."

"Yeah, no kidding."

Chris barely kept from jerking around to stare at him. What was that supposed to mean? Was he comparing her unfavorably to Eva?

She scoffed. Who cared? Unless and until he was actually her brother-in-law, she was indifferent. In fact, she was not interested in discussing Eva or herself with him. Or interested in discussing anything with him. She wanted to go home and pull the covers over her head and have a good cry. Maybe punch something.

"But you're liking it here?"

"Sure." Chris was exasperated. Did he not get the hint when she answered with monosyllables or didn't answer at all that she was not interested in talking to him?

"Nice weather anyway." He was watching her, she could tell, and it made her want to fidget. Actually it made her want to put her hand out and push his manly jaw away so he could check out Gus instead and she could have peace. "But slow, quiet. I imagine you're so used to going one hundred percent that you sometimes feel like you're falling behind."

Chris glanced over sharply, then away, because she didn't want to meet his eyes for some reason. He had this sort of...forceful stare, which was too personal or something.

But the truth was, she *had* been feeling like that, especially at the shop. During the early-morning rush—which wasn't much of a rush at all compared to the crowds at NYEspresso—she was astounded at customers' patience, especially when people in line wanted a manual pour, which could take as long as five minutes per cup. At that hour people in New York wanted their coffee and they wanted to leave, one, two, done, to sprint to the office, to catch a train, to get to a meeting. Chris had nearly gone out of her mind the first morning she'd worked alone at Slow Pour when what she'd consider an unacceptably long line had formed. But no one had seemed to mind the wait; they'd stood patiently and chatted, complimented her on her coffee, wished her a nice day, or peace or to be well.

It was nice, she guessed, but definitely…foreign. Zac had nailed it. "I do feel a little out of tempo sometimes."

"Kind of a strange adjustment to have to make, huh."

How did he know? Chris sighed. She might as well ask him. At least talking to him was better than staring out at Mr. Love Me Love My Board. "Sounds like you've done something similar?"

He didn't answer for so long she turned and found him staring at her, a half smile on his lips. A tingle of excitement ran down her spine. Argh! For heaven's sake! Was she that starved for attention? "What is so funny?"

"Nothing. I'm just glad you decided it was okay to talk to me."

"Oh. Right." She poked at a piece of seaweed in the sand to avoid looking at him again. He saw way too much, and it was really annoying. "I have been in a better mood."

"No worries. To answer your question, I served as a Peace Corps volunteer in Africa. Big transition going over. Big transition back."

Okay. That was unexpected. Somehow she'd pictured him springing full-grown out of one of the Slow Pour chairs and doing nothing else. Had Eva ever mentioned anything else about him? Whatever she'd said, Chris had taken it as shorthand for "beach bum." Nothing about him until now had contradicted that impression. "That must have been an incredible experience. Life changing."

"Yup. So I get what you're going through."

"Come on." Chris waved away that concept. "You changed countries, cultures, *everything*. I just changed states. Boohoo."

"Change is hard." He reached over and touched her arm, his blue eyes kind. "You're allowed to find this rough sometimes, Chris."

To her horror, tears threatened; she had to swallow hard. What was this, PMS? She was never, ever this fragile.

"When did you last eat?" He was again studying her carefully, could probably tell she was struggling. The guy's intuition and perceptiveness creeped her out. She felt like a cell on a microscope slide.

"I had some… I don't know." She sniffed and tossed back her hair, pretending to enjoy the breeze.

Next to her, rustling sounds. He was digging something out of his bag. "Here. Cashew-granola-cranberry bars. I make them myself. I brought plenty."

"You cook?" She was on the verge of refusing one, but quite honestly, the red-studded bars wrapped tightly in plastic wrap looked chewy and delicious, and she was really hungry, having stupidly assumed she and Gus would be getting something to eat.

"Sure. These are good for energy. Here." He held out a thermos. "Have some of this, too."

"Not until you tell me what it is." She bit into the bar—it was nutty, chewy, not too sweet, with the gift of a few surprise mini chocolate chips. "Mmm, these are fabulous, thank you."

"No problem." He held out the thermos, eyes twinkling. "The smoothie is a secret recipe. Trust me?"

"Why should I?"

"Because it's California and that's what you do here."

Chris rolled her eyes good-naturedly, took the thermos and peeked in. "It's green."

"Uh-huh."

She sniffed. Frowned. Took a sip. The flavors were creamy and complex. "Whoa, what is that? Mint? Banana? Ginger?"

"All of the above. You have good taste buds. There's more, too."

She eyed him suspiciously. "How much more?"

"Kale, cilantro, pineapple, hemp seeds—"

"*Kale?* Yeah, okay. I get it. Disgustingly good for me." She took another sip, feeling better already, and handed back the thermos. "And delicious. Thank you again, Zac."

"Sure." He grinned at her, then chuckled.

"What?"

"That's the first time you've said my name."

"Uh." Chris stared incredulously. "You kept track?"

He shrugged, raising the thermos to his lips.

The guy better not be crushing on her. She had zero interest.

And who put *vegetables* in a smoothie, anyway?

They sat in silence for a while, Zac apparently contentedly watching the waves roll in, Chris nearly twitching from the silence between them. She hated silence.

"So…what you do when you're not at Slow Pour?"

He was clearly amused again. As if he got that she was finally talking to him only because she found the silence so awkward. "I'm finishing my degree."

Ah, so he was a student. He must have gone back to finish now, a bunch of years after dropping out—she'd put him in his early thirties. Well, good for him, better late than never. "In what?"

"Engineering. Specialization in water engineering."

"Wow. So you'll end up with a bachelor of science degree for that? Pretty technical for undergrad."

His smile was slow and smug. "This would be for my master's."

Oh, crap. She bit her lip. "I see. So then…"

"Are you trying to figure out why I'm at the café so much? If I'm a poor slob or independently wealthy? Where I've been all your life?"

Chris shrugged irritably, as if she didn't care, when in fact that was exactly what she had been trying to figure out. "Something like that. And also not."

He laughed. "If you want to ask me something, Chris, just ask."

"Why do I have to do all the work?" She scowled good-naturedly. "If you know I want to know something, just *tell* me."

Zac chuckled, conceding the point. "Okay. Let's see. I went to UC Berkeley undergrad, worked for an engineering firm for several years before and after the Peace Corps. This fall I'm finishing my master's at Cal Poly in San Luis Obispo and applying to doctoral programs for next year. Ultimately I want to teach."

Holy— Chris gaped at his peaceful profile. She'd stuffed Zac safely away in the beach-bum category, rich or poor didn't matter, and now she found out he was not only intelligent, but ambitious, with clear goals and a plan. For some reason the surprise of him annoyed her all over again. Why hadn't Eva ever told her this?

Come on. That wasn't her sister's fault. Chris had made the stupid and rather snotty assumptions all by herself.

"Dude!" Gus waded toward them in the fading light,

backlit by the magenta ball of the setting sun. "Is that one of your kale smoothies?"

"Sure is." Zac got to his feet as Gus came closer. They high-fived, then fist-bumped. Chris snorted. *Seriously, dudes, just shake hands and get over yourselves.* At least they didn't bounce their chests off each other.

She was so done with this roller-coaster evening, and with the strain of talking to Zac, not feeling sure of herself around him. Frankly, she hated it.

"How'd you like the surfing?" Gus unzipped his wet suit to his navel and pulled down the hood, smiling triumphantly.

How did *she* like it? "Oh, it was great. You looked great out there. I guess. I mean, to be honest, I wouldn't know."

Zac shot her yet another amused look. She hated him. He should not be standing there enjoying her misery.

"Yeah, it's the best. I'm good. You can trust me on that. Right, bro?" He reached to high-five Zac *again*.

God give her strength.

"So, Chris." Gus beamed at her, water dripping off his bangs, teeth shining, bare chest gleaming through the unzipped wet suit. Okay, she was still pissed, but because he was physically perfect, he could still save the evening if he suggested right now that they do something romantic and wonderful. "How about driving to San Luis Obispo to shoot some pool?"

Nope. That was not romantic. At least not to her. "I don't play pool."

"Excellent!" Once again, her total lack of enthusiasm didn't faze him at all. "I can teach you."

"No." She bared her teeth in a vicious smile. "I mean I *don't*...play...pool. Like, ever."

"Oh." He blew out a quick breath, glanced back and

forth between her and Zac a few times, rocking on his heels. "Awkward!"

Zac decided this was a good time to crouch and pack up his bag. He was undoubtedly right.

Chris closed her eyes. Okay. She needed to behave better. Her current mood was not all Gus's fault. She'd agreed to "hang out" with him, that was all. They'd both come to this in good faith, just with radically different expectations.

"Pool's not my thing, Gus. Why don't we do something else? Have dinner, catch a movie or a concert..."

"Oh." Gus's brows drew down. "See, some of my friends are meeting us at this place to shoot pool. I told them we'd be there."

"Ah." Chris smiled sweetly, already out of renewed patience.

"Listen, you guys have fun. I gotta get going." Zac nodded to Gus and gave Chris a smirk that made her want to slug him. His smirk turned into a full grin, which meant he could probably tell she wanted to slug him, which made her want to slug him even harder.

He turned and started off, broad shoulders swinging, long legs eating up the sand even with his slow stride. Chris suffered a quick and unwelcome pang of panic, as if her lifeline to civilization as she knew it was being slowly stretched until it frayed and severed.

She turned to Gus, unnerved and exhausted. "Maybe you should just drive me home and we can make plans another night."

"Yeah. So." Gus tapped his sports watch, grimacing apologetically. "That's kind of the opposite direction. We're going to be late already."

Chris stood frozen, blinking at him. Okay. So far she'd

been willing to admit that part of this disaster was her fault.

Not that part.

She glanced at Zac's back. For God's sake, now she'd have to ask him a favor. "Maybe Zac will take me home."

"Listen, Chris." Gus touched her arm, his fingers still chilled from the water. "I'm sorry. I messed this up. See, you kind of intimidate me, being classier and everything. I guess surfing and friends felt safer. But it was sort of a dumb idea for a date with someone like you. You're not my usual type. But I think you're amazing. I really do."

Chris turned from preparing to launch herself into a sprint after Zac. Gus was standing with his head hanging down, that gorgeous body molded in the wet suit, the sun setting behind him. He looked like something out of a catalog.

Her frosty mood thawed. "Aw, Gus. It's okay. Really. We just had different ideas about tonight."

"So it's okay if I call you again?" He lifted his head hopefully. "It might be awhile. I've got a surf competition down in Huntington Beach in a few days."

"Sure." She put her hand on his solid forearm and squeezed, then glanced anxiously after Zac again.

"Yo, Zac!" Gus's voice nearly burst her eardrums. Way up the beach, Zac turned.

"Okay, you're good." Gus gave her a gentle shove. "We'll talk soon."

She sent one more smile into his Greek-god face and ran off to catch her ride from the irritating titan.

7

AMES AVOIDED NYESPRESSO on his way home from a meeting with a potential client restaurateur and chef. He was in a terrible mood, and not stopping in to get a cup of coffee made him even crankier. The meeting hadn't gone as well as it should have. The restaurant owner had been stringing Ames along for weeks, and the chef was one of those massive egos Ames could usually work around, but today he wasn't in the mood. Yes, he got that the chef's reputation was on the line when a new place opened; yes, he got that some people dealt with anxiety by becoming giant buttheads. *Zee world, she is not always going to be your escargot, monsieur. Get over it.*

Bottom line, Ames sold excellent wine at reasonable prices from a house with decades of a spotless high-end reputation. The stuff should sell itself, and usually it did.

The worst part?

He couldn't stop thinking about Eva.

Again.

Still.

This was not supposed to happen! More to the point, this never *did* happen. He either fell in love with women early on and violently, or he didn't. Nice and simple. If he did fall, he'd pursue and/or date her for a week, a month, a year or several years, until the problems became obvious and the relationship dissolved. Then he'd grieve and move on. One-night stands didn't bother him if they didn't bother whoever. Short relationships, long relationships, he'd had them all, and prided himself on pretty much every one ending pleasantly. Yes, he'd like to have something work out forever, get himself settled down and have a family. But that hadn't happened yet, and he was fine waiting until he found the right woman.

Then along came Eva. He hadn't fallen in love with her early on and violently. In fact, he'd found her pretty exasperating, slightly embarrassing, utterly charming, but not someone he could ever see himself falling for or dating seriously. After she'd shown up naked in his shower—an image he had not been able to get out of his mind—he figured being up-front about that early on was the smartest thing he could do for both of them.

One night, then draw the line, because what was the point of going further?

The problem was that their one night had only left him feeling as if something was missing, that there was more he wanted, more of her to explore, a lot of unfinished business still between them. Not to mention he'd been walking around half-hard for the past four days thinking about her.

His phone rang. He dug it out of his pocket and checked the display. His brother, Mike. "Hey, Mickey."

"S'up? Where are you?"

"On my way home. Where are you?"

"Walking down Park Avenue."

Ames rolled his eyes, battling a jolt of annoyance. His brother did this all the time. "Why didn't you tell me you were coming into town?"

"I did tell you. I sent you an email last week. Got any plans tonight?"

Mike was notorious for this, too. He'd *meant* to email Ames last week, and in his brain that probably counted. But okay, Ames wasn't doing anything, and seeing his younger brother would cheer him up. Or at least keep him from more useless mooning over a woman totally wrong for him. "I'm free. What are you thinking?"

"I'm meeting Josh for dinner later, but I'm having drinks with you first at that bar we went to last time— Old Town, near Union Square."

"What time?" He already knew the answer. *Now.*

"Now. I'm turning onto Eighteenth Street. Get here soon."

"All right. Be there in twenty."

Twenty-five minutes later, he was hugging and back-slapping his younger brother, Mike, in town on a school break to see friends from college. He'd stayed in New Jersey teaching middle-school science in Hopewell, a pretty little town near Princeton. Ames admired his brother's dedication and patience, especially given that Mike had grown up with neither, but Ames would rather clean bathrooms for a living than face a class of adolescents every day.

They found stools at the long, elegant bar and ordered draft beers and French fries to share, their favorite snack from childhood—back then substituting Cokes for beer.

"How's school going?"

Mike broke into a grin. "It's crazed. These kids are so high on hormones it's all I can do to keep them sitting still. I'm like their teacher-policeman. At the same time, when they click in, when they get what I'm teaching, what I'm trying to communicate about their bodies, about the earth and how things work, it's the best."

"Excellent." Ames toasted him. "You are braver than I am. Speaking of brave, how is Julie feeling?"

"Much better, or I wouldn't be here now. She had a terrible first trimester. I can't believe she managed on a full teaching load. She'll be a great mom."

He spoke with adoring pride. Julie was indomitable, the only force known to man who could have gotten Ames's brother to settle down after a turbulent child-hood of self-destructive rebellion. Married four years, they were absolutely crazy about each other and expect-ing their first child in early March.

For the first time Ames's usual pleasure over Mike's happiness was tainted with a new emotion, a darker one—irritation or…envy?

An image of Eva came into his mind, her lips parted, her body held tight, seconds before it released into or-gasm. Then Eva again, smiling into his eyes as he stroked her belly, swelling with their unborn—

Good God, what had they put in his beer? He'd had that fantasy once before, about six months into a promis-ing relationship, which had ended abruptly when—

"Yo, Ames. What is *up?*"

"Huh?" He started, coming back to the bar and to his brother, embarrassed to be caught daydreaming. "What? What are you talking about?"

Mike stared at him suspiciously. "You got this really goofy look on your face."

"I did not."

"Dude. Big-time. What's that about? You seeing some-one? That woman I met last time is history, right? The icy brunette—what was her name?"

"Taylor." He shoved in a handful of French fries, washed it down with beer. Yeah, Taylor was brilliant, unbearably sexy, but *icy* was a good word. Mike had un-canny instincts. Kind of like Eva. "No, I'm not seeing her anymore. There's no one."

"There is *someone*. C'mon, I know you better than that. What's up with her? Trouble?"

Ames sighed. His brother wouldn't give up, and he might as well talk these weird feelings out with someone he trusted.

"I met this woman. Eva. She's…I don't know, a little crazy. Not in a bad way—maybe *unusual* is a better word. Certainly she's not like any woman I've ever dated. Not that I'm dating her." He laughed, then realized there was nothing funny about what he was saying; he was just babbling like a nervous dork, so he shut up. "She seems to get that I'm not interested, but she keeps showing up and getting me to do things I have no intention of doing, like playing mini golf in a bar where there were these huge plastic zoo animals everywhere. Can you imagine me doing that?"

"Nope." Mike was smirking. Ames hated it when Mike smirked. "If you told me any of your women demanded dinner in Paris, yes, but mini golf with zoo animals? Nope. Tell me more."

"First of all, she's not my woman. But anyway, she shows up at my condo with dinner one night—uninvited, this is, like, the third time I've ever seen her—and then she just walks in while I'm taking a *shower,* and…well, you know." He shoved in more French fries, feeling guilty, as if he'd betrayed Eva by talking about it, which annoyed him, because he owed her nothing. Not as if they were dating.

"Ooh." Mike's eyebrows rose over his smirk. "A naked, willing woman in the shower. What a *nightmare.*"

"Yeah, yeah, I know." Ames gulped more beer. Somehow this was not coming out the way he'd intended. "Well, it was weird. So I told her that was it, it was just that night."

"And she's been stalking you?"

"No." More French fries. More beer. And another fry. Or two. "She was fine with it."

"So…you meet a woman who isn't your type, you tell her to go away, she does, and…" Mike held out his hand. "I don't get it. What's the problem?"

Ames gritted his teeth. "I can't stop thinking about her."

"Sorry?" Mike put a hand to his ear, speaking too loudly, enjoying himself hugely. "I'm sorry, what was that? You can't what? Can't stop thinking about her? Was that what you said? You weren't quite clear."

Ames forced his jaw to relax. "You heard me."

"Ooh." Mike was having way too much fun. "It sounds like this woman has you a little off balance, maybe? A little confused? Don't know which way is up? Eating French fries uncontrollably?"

Ames took back his hand, which had been reaching for more. "It's not a big deal."

"No, no, of *course* not." Mike nodded with exaggerated slowness. Still smirking. "I have a theory, but it will piss you off."

"Then I don't want to hear it."

"Okay. Then I'll be kind and simply say go with your feelings, Ames. You feel like seeing her? See her. You don't? Don't. You've been honest with her. Keep doing that, but also be honest with yourself and you can't mess up."

Ames squinted at him. "That was way too easy."

"I'm serious. That's all there is. You just gotta wait and it will all figure itself out." He slapped Ames on the back. "I have to say, man, this is great to see, however."

"What is?" Ames was pretty sure he didn't want to know.

"A woman who's got you totally messed up." He chuck-led madly. "I am loving it. *Nothing* messes you up. Nothing ever *has* messed you up. And now this woman has *messed...you...up!*"

"Very funny." Okay, so Ames had always been the predictable straight guy in the family. It was serious business being the oldest son, especially when your brother had majored in falling apart. "What kind of season you think the Browns will end up with this year?"

The tactic worked, same way it always did. Once his brother got talking football, that was it. In fact, usually Ames tried to hold the subject off until he got a sense of how his brother was doing. This time, he needed the intervention.

They chatted pleasantly until Mike had to leave for his dinner appointment. Ames considered having another beer, but though he generally didn't mind having a drink on his own, tonight it didn't feel right.

He paid the tab and stepped out of the restaurant. The temperature had dropped; the air had become damp and penetrating, smelling of approaching rain. He was nearly to the Union Square subway station when his phone rang.

Eva.

Now what? His attempt at righteous exasperation was hijacked by a thrill of pleasure seeing her name. Which irritated the hell out of him.

"Hey, Eva." He kept his voice curt. "What's up?"

"Hi. Um…are you home right now?" She didn't sound like herself. Her voice was low, dispirited. Ames went on immediate alert.

"I'm on my way back, why?"

"Oh, then, never mind."

"No, I'll be there in twenty minutes. What's going

on?" His heart was beating faster. He sped his steps toward the subway entrance.

"Look, it's nothing, really. This guy came into the café about half an hour ago, drunk off his ass. He gave me the creeps. I just closed the store, and I think I see him outside. I don't want to call the police, I mean, he hasn't done anything, but I also don't want to—"

"Stay in the café." He broke into a jog. "Wait for me. Don't go out or try anything, okay?"

"No, no. Jeez, now I feel stupid, I'm probably totally overreacting."

"You're not overreacting. You're being smart. Stay there. I'm on my way."

"Thank you. Really." Her relief made him feel like superman.

Miraculously a train was just arriving when he got to the platform. He was first out of the car at Forty-Second Street and half ran the half mile to Tenth Avenue, thinking if this was another of Eva's tricks to spend time with him, he'd be able to indulge his righteous exasperation genuinely, and then some.

She wasn't kidding. A guy was pacing unsteadily back and forth opposite NYEspresso, watching the shop intently. He was around forty, short, skinny, hair wild, clothes baggy and mismatched, and not warm enough for the chilly evening.

Ames turned hot with anger. Taking a deep breath, he walked up to the guy, not sure if he was being brave or stupid. Probably both. "Hey, you waiting for someone?"

"None of your business."

"I'm Ames." He offered to shake. "What's your name?"

"Stan." The guy glared his hand. "Stanley."

"Hi, Stanley." Ames put his hand back in his coat pocket. "You see the woman in the coffee shop there?"

Stanley turned to stare suspiciously.

"Yeah, not sure if you were hoping for a chance there, but she's with me."

"I don't give a flying—"

"Right. Well, good, then." He kept his tone friendly. "But if she calls me again and tells me you're harassing her, we're putting police on speed dial, okay?"

The guy's face crumpled with anger and embarrassment. "Hey, man, screw you."

"Okay, good. We're good, then." Ames held up his hands. "Just a misunderstanding."

Stanley sent him a withering glare. "Man, she *deserves* a jerk like you."

"Yeah, she probably does." Ames nodded pleasantly. "Nice talking to you."

Stanley walked off in disgust. When he turned the corner onto Forty-Fourth Street without looking back or slowing, Ames's body started to relax, adrenaline slacking off.

He crossed the street to NYEspresso, catching Eva's worried face peeking through the front window of the dim shop. He gave her a thumbs-up, feeling like a hero returning home victorious after an epic battle, aware since his fight-or-flight instinct had calmed down that confronting a drunk, hostile guy had probably been really stupid.

She opened the door. "Ames. Thank you so much. I can't believe you did that."

"It was nothing. I was on my way home anyway. No big deal." He resisted the urge to swagger and puff out his chest. Women made men act like complete morons. "But if you see him again, call the police immediately, okay?"

"Yes. I will." She still looked pale.

Another rush of protectiveness. He wanted to bring

her up to his place, calm her down, feed her, make her feel safe…

Yeah, then what? It wasn't his job to take care of her. He'd made his decision regarding their lack of a future, and if he was going to change his mind, it wasn't going to be on a dark night when he was still feeling shaky himself.

She came out into the street and locked the door behind her, fumbling with the keys. Her hands were trembling.

Ames would hail her a cab, pay for her to go home. No way was he letting her take the subway.

He opened his mouth to offer. Made a strangled sound. The words wouldn't come.

Eva looked up at him, startled, searching his face, vulnerable and sweet. She was wearing zebra-striped leggings and a patchwork tunic over red high-tops. Her hair was gathered in a clump of curls on one side of her head and decorated with black-and-pink plastic snails. Instead of weird, the outfit struck him as incredibly endearing.

He took a breath, ready to try again. Cab. Home. He could do this.

"Why don't you come up to my place for a drink? You look like you could use one."

No, no, what happened? Those were the wrong words.

"Oh." Eva blinked, clearly taken aback. "That would actually be really nice, Ames. I'm not up for a commute just yet. Thank you for understanding."

"Sure." He hated seeing her so subdued. He hated how much he wanted to pull her into his arms and kiss her, make her smile again, make her laugh, restart her crazy energy.

Instead, he took her hand and kept it all the way up to his place, where he let go reluctantly, because it would be seriously weird to keep holding it walking around his condo.

"What do you feel like?" He moved into the kitchen, which was bright and warm and smelled of Jean's earlier cooking. Exactly the homey atmosphere he wanted to offer her right now. "Wine? Beer? Harder stuff?"

"Wine is fine." She stopped in the doorway, as if still uncommitted to being home alone with him. "Red or white, whatever's open."

"You hungry?" He removed a covered dish from the refrigerator. "Jean made lasagna."

"I am sort of hungry. If you're sure…"

"Sure that it's lasagna?" He quirked an eyebrow, relieved when she smiled. "Yes, I'm sure."

"Thanks, Ames." She hugged her arms around herself, tightening the baggy top to her slender frame, exposing the tiny hummingbird at her neck. "This is really nice of you. I was a little shaken up."

"Yeah?" He slid the lasagna into the microwave and turned it on. "Why, they don't have weirdos in California?"

"Ha-ha." She nodded when he held up a bottle of Valpolicella. "They have plenty."

"Just none in your shop."

"Actually." She waited so long to continue that he had the wine open and the bottle ready to pour before he looked up questioningly. "It wasn't the guy so much. It was you walking right up to him. He could have had a gun, Ames. He could have been high or mentally ill. He could have hurt you or killed you. All because of my paranoia."

Ames put the bottle down. She was breathing high and shallow, blue eyes wide with worry. A tear rolled down her right cheek.

He was stunned.

Then nearly overwhelmed by tenderness.

"Hey." He poured her wine and offered it awkwardly, realizing how stupid it was to offer her a drink when all he wanted was to hold her. "It's okay. I'm okay."

"I know." She laughed briefly, wiped another tear and stepped into the kitchen to accept her glass. "But if I knew you were going to be such a dumb ass I would have just called the police."

"Dumb ass! *Me?*" He jerked his thumb to his chest, pretending outrage. "I was the ultimate hero out there. Thor, Iron Man *and* Captain America combined!"

"Okay, ultimate hero. And dumb ass."

He rolled his eyes and poured himself wine, still shaken by her emotions—and his in response. "Okay, maybe it wasn't the best idea. But it worked out."

"It did. And thank you, Ames." She held up her glass to his. "I should have sounded more grateful, I was just terrified."

"No worries." He clinked with her, smiling at her over the rim, and took a sip, expecting her to do the same.

Instead, she lowered her head for a few moments, then lifted her gaze back to his, blue and warm and deeply vulnerable.

His smile faded. His heart seemed too big for his chest, was pounding too strongly.

Only the microwave's obnoxious beep-beep-beeping saved him from kissing her.

If he kissed her, he'd want to kiss her again. And again. They'd end up in his bedroom. For that step, he needed his brain and intentions clear. Around Eva tonight, they were neither.

"Dinner's on."

"I'll get silverware." She put her glass on the counter

and opened the drawer where he kept his plastic wrap and foil. "As soon as I remember where it is."

"That one." He pointed to the drawer next to the sink. "Get spoons, too, if you want ice cream for dessert. Mint chocolate chip. Very healthy. Mint is a vegetable, right?"

She giggled, first one all night, music to his ears. "Practically salad."

"Then we're set."

They took their dishes to the dining room, a pleasant room that Ames pretty much never used. When he had friends over, they went out or ordered in and set up in the living room. He wasn't much for formal entertaining at home. With all the restaurants in New York, you didn't have to be.

"This is really nice wine. Is it one of yours?"

He nodded. "Yeah, I stomped the grapes in the basement last year."

"I knew it." She plunked both elbows on the table. "I was thinking about you visiting vineyards and how I bet it's like visiting coffee plantations. There's this really elemental connection to the beverage that you miss when you just buy the finished product in a store, you know? So much natural beauty that exists even in these highly cultivated plantings. And there are so many people involved, working so hard to make the plants flourish, the harvest successful, the processing of highest quality for the best end result."

"Yes." He understood exactly what she meant. He'd felt the same awe, the same respect for the natural and man-made power that went into the ruby liquid in his glass.

"Coffee flowers smell fabulous, too. Like jasmine." Her expression turned wistful, distant. "I remember being completely enchanted by the smell as a girl. And they're so beautiful."

YOUR PARTICIPATION IS REQUESTED!

Dear Reader,

Since you are a lover of our books – we would like to get to know you!

Inside you will find a short Reader's Survey. Sharing your answers with us will help our editorial staff understand who you are and what activities you enjoy.

To thank you for your participation, we would like to send you 2 books and 2 gifts – **ABSOLUTELY FREE!**

Enjoy your gifts with our appreciation,

Pam Powers

SEE INSIDE FOR READER'S SURVEY

For Your Reading Pleasure...

We'll send you 2 books and 2 gifts
ABSOLUTELY FREE
just for completing our Reader's Survey!

YOUR READER'S SURVEY
"THANK YOU" FREE GIFTS INCLUDE:
- ▶ **2 FREE books**
- ▶ **2 lovely surprise gifts**

PLEASE FILL IN THE CIRCLES COMPLETELY TO RESPOND

1) What type of fiction books do you enjoy reading? (Check all that apply)
- ○ Suspense/Thrillers ○ Action/Adventure ○ Modern-day Romances
- ○ Historical Romance ○ Humour ○ Paranormal Romance

2) What attracted you most to the last fiction book you purchased on impulse?
- ○ The Title ○ The Cover ○ The Author ○ The Story

3) What is usually the greatest influencer when you <u>plan</u> to buy a book?
- ○ Advertising ○ Referral ○ Book Review

4) How often do you access the internet?
- ○ Daily ○ Weekly ○ Monthly ○ Rarely or never

5) How many NEW paperback fiction novels have you purchased in the past 3 months?
- ○ 0 - 2 ○ 3 - 6 ○ 7 or more

YES! I have completed the Reader's Survey. Please send me the 2 FREE books and 2 FREE gifts (gifts are worth about $10) for which I qualify. I understand that I am under no obligation to purchase any books, as explained on the back of this card.

150/350 HDL GF9S

FIRST NAME	LAST NAME

ADDRESS

APT.#	CITY

STATE/PROV.	ZIP/POSTAL CODE

EMAIL

HB-914-SUR-13

"Grape flowers smell more...herbal, I guess. And frankly they look like a bunch of broccoli."

Eva giggled, sipped her wine. Her color was back to its usual healthy pink, but she was still subdued. "Where were you when I called?"

"At a bar near Union Square. The place we almost got to. Good beer, nice place."

"Who—" She ducked her head and forked up more lasagna. "Lucky for me you were on your way back."

His heart squeezed. Was she thinking he'd been on a date? Did it upset her? Maybe he should let her think that. It might be easier all around...

Aw, hell. "My brother, Mike, called. He was in town seeing friends, so we met for a drink."

"Oh, that's nice." She nodded, her smile returning. "My sister is about my favorite person to spend time with. Are you close to Mike?"

"Better now." He put down his wineglass. "He went through some tough years. A few brushes with illegal substances and the law."

"While you were driving the getaway car?"

"Oh, yeah, that was me." He nodded solemnly. "Living on the edge, same as I do now."

She contemplated her glass, frowning thoughtfully, making Ames want to smooth the furrows from her forehead. "Did you ever feel like he got all the attention?"

Her comment took him aback. She'd hit it, absolutely. "Why do you say that?"

"My sister and me. You'd never believe it to look at me, but I was more of a rebel than Chris."

"No way. I would have picked her as the bad girl."

"I know, right? But it was me. I cut school, tried to fail a few courses, hung out with a wild crowd, had just a few issues conforming to expectations, yadda yadda."

He just laughed. "Uh-huh."

"I think Chris felt as if I did all that for the spotlight, instead of what it really was."

"What was it?"

She frowned, looking perplexed. "I'm not exactly sure. Probably partly basic wiring. But it's also really hard to be born into a close family and feel like you're the only one who is different. I suppose some people react by suppressing their differences to fit in better. I did the opposite. Anyway, it took Chris and me a while to work it out. But we did."

"We did, too. In the meantime Mike settled down, got a good job, married a great woman. They have a kid on the way." He stared at his plate, wondering at this urge to unburden himself tonight. Maybe Jean had made a Lasagna of Truth. "I had goals, things I wanted to accomplish, life plans. I was self-sufficient. So I guess I did feel at times as if I took second place to his bad behavior."

"Hmm." Eva regarded him thoughtfully. "So what you're saying is that your brother was a sexy rebel and you were an uptight little nerd."

"Yes." He nodded enthusiastically. "Yes, that's it exactly."

Her smile turned wicked. The sparkle returned to her eyes. "You poor guy. No wonder mini golf was so traumatic. I should have suggested a library trip. We could have hung out in the reference section."

"Oh, *yeah*." He sent her a smoldering look. "And have you read me the dictionary?"

"Ha!" She threw him a look and finished her lasagna. He was glad to see her relaxing enough to eat well. He'd barely touched his. Nervous. Unsettled.

And, oh, yeah, all those French fries.

"So what about your family? Are your parents more like you or Chris?"

"Like Chris. Numbers, charts, schedules…and there was me, freak child." She rolled her eyes. "I'm surprised they didn't auction me off on eBay."

"I would have bought you." The words slipped out more seriously than he'd intended.

She looked startled, then blew a mischievous raspberry. "Yeah, I'll bet. And you'd take me to your fancy dinners and parties and insist I wear this very outfit."

An awkward silence passed while he tried to imagine Eva as his date to Boyce Wines's client dinner at La Grenouille Laide at the end of the month. He'd taken Taylor the previous year, and had to admit that he'd been pumped showing up with the hottest woman in the room, but their relationship had already turned dysfunctional. "Why, would you *want* to go with me to fancy dinners?"

"*No,* I wouldn't want to go with you. Jeez. I'd be completely out of place."

"Oh." Her rejection startled him with its intensity. "Okay."

More awkwardness.

"Hey." Eva touched his sleeve, worried and subdued again. "I'm sorry. I assumed you were teasing me."

"Yeah, I was." He glared down at his plate. The Lasagna of Truth had failed him. He'd only been half teasing. Or maybe…

Damn it, he had no idea. His brother was right, the woman had *messed…him…up!*

"Well, because—"

"Why, do you—"

They stopped, each waiting for the other to break the stalemate.

Then they started laughing.

"Okay. I think we'll drop that topic." Eva drained her glass and stood with her empty plate. "Thanks so much for the rescue tonight. I should get going. Early shift tomorrow."

"Sure." Ames stood slowly, startled by her abrupt announcement and his realization that he wasn't ready to let her go. He thought she'd want to finish the bottle with him, maybe sit in the living room, light a fire...

And?

Aw, hell. He still wanted her. In fact, he wanted her more now than he had the night she'd shown up naked in his shower. He wasn't sure what had happened in the intervening days. He hadn't seen her, hadn't spoken to her. Maybe it was just that tonight had been more intimate. They'd shared fear, shared relief, shared some of their vulnerabilities, their family and job experiences. He felt as if they'd been dancing toward something inevitable.

Apparently he'd been dancing alone.

"Okay." He took his plate into the kitchen, loaded the dishwasher while she put away the lasagna leftovers and recorked the wine.

It felt good hanging out with her again.

He should at least go down with her and get her a cab.

He opened his mouth to offer.

"Do you want to spend the night?"

8

Do you want to spend the night?

Eva was glad she couldn't see herself just then, because she was undoubtedly looking as if someone had hit her over the head with a brick. She *could* see Ames, however, and it was obvious he'd hit himself with the same brick, stunned by asking nearly as much as he'd stunned her. Maybe he hadn't meant to ask, but he wanted her to stay. Instinct always won out.

A few days ago, she would have taken his request as a victory—aha! She'd called it! The one night they'd had together hadn't been enough.

But tonight something had changed. She hadn't expected the degree of sweetness and tenderness Ames would exhibit when she'd felt so threatened. Or the way he'd rushed in to protect her without asking questions, for all he knew putting his life on the line.

Even more startling were her emotions when she'd thought Drunk Creepy Guy might hurt him. Eva had been beyond terrified, approaching panic. Several men had made their way into her heart, and every single time she'd been hopeful something wonderful and lasting would come out of the relationship. But when nothing did, she was philosophical, focusing on how much she had enjoyed the guys, the sex, the company and the thrill of a new romance.

Never had she felt that if her chance ever to be with any of them again ended decisively, her entire world could explode. Even now, a couple of hours later, understanding that the emotions sprang from a moment of extreme stress, possible danger—not at all the norm of her previous dating life—she was still uneasy, unsettled, a little wobbly, as if one strong push could send her toppling.

Into what or where, she had no idea.

Did she want to spend the night with Ames? Yes. It would save her a vulnerable-feeling trip back into the dark and cold, and she could sleep a little later in the morning before she had to be at work.

And yes, after her scare, she wouldn't mind being in a pair of strong male arms tonight, particularly those belonging to Ames.

And yes, she'd wanted their affair to resume, had counted on it, really, even when he'd insisted they were stopping after one night.

But—and she couldn't believe she was thinking this—tonight for some reason home seemed…safer. Even with nutty Natalie around.

"The guest room is made up." Ames pointed to the third bedroom. "It's no trouble."

Oh. Guest room. Oops.

Eva sighed, a combination of relief and, yeah, a little disappointment—even if she'd been considering turning him down, who didn't want to be wanted? So Ames wasn't changing his mind about drawing the line at one night with her. At least, not yet. That was okay. In fact, emotionally it was probably better. She'd be able to put this disorienting evening behind her and wake up back to her old indomitable self. "Thanks, Ames. I would have been fine, but I admit I wasn't excited about going out there again. It's nice of you to offer."

"You're welcome." He looked vaguely troubled.

She forced a smile. "In fact, you have been the most remarkable knight in shining armor all night, and I so appreciate it."

"You're welcome again." He rubbed his hand over his face. "Do you need anything? A toothbrush? Pajamas?"

"Just a toothbrush." She wasn't above hoping he was imagining her sleeping naked. Tonight wasn't their night, but that didn't mean there wouldn't be another shot, after she'd calmed down and regained her healthy perspective.

"There should be a new one in the bathroom mirror cabinet next to your room. The towels in there are clean, too." He stood there, still looking troubled, as if there was something he still needed to do or say.

She was tired.

"Good night, Ames." Eva put her arms around him for a fierce hug. "Thank you again for being my hero tonight."

"Sleep well." His arms came solidly around her, preventing her from keeping the hug brief. "I'm sorry I scared you."

"It's okay." She made the mistake of looking up at him. His brown eyes were intense, holding hers, one eyebrow quirked questioningly. Her instinct translated immediately, making her heart hammer in her chest. Ames might have offered the guest room, but he still wanted her.

Eva still wanted him, too.

Smiling blandly, she stepped back, gave a little wave and went into the guest bathroom, closed the door and leaned against it.

Whoa. She needed to get a grip. First her instinct said no, now it was saying yes. A good night's sleep would take care of the weirdness. She'd be back on track and they could return to the fun fling she'd wanted, which he did, too, though he hadn't admitted it yet out loud.

Then she could go home to California and hang out until it was time to marry Zac. Because this whole intensely angsty, wildly vulnerable ride she'd been on over Ames tonight was not her thing at all.

Settled.

She took care of her business, brushed her teeth and decided on a quick shower. Five minutes later, she came out of the bathroom and headed toward the guest room, wrapped in a towel.

Across the living room in the master bedroom, Ames had just emerged from his bathroom, torso naked, towel wrapped around his hips.

She stopped short.

So did he.

Silence except for her high, quick breaths.

His hands came off his hips. The towel dropped.

Uh-oh.

He walked toward her, his eyes not leaving hers.

Double uh-oh.

No, no, this was fine. She'd just explain to him that, um, she was… That he…

Oh, my God, he was so handsome. Eva was crazy about him. She wanted him. Her instinct was not only green-lighting, but waving checkered flags, *go go go go go*.

This was how she rolled.

She let go of her towel and met him in the middle, arms sliding around his neck, welcoming the warmth of his skin against hers in the cool room.

He felt perfect.

She stood still, eyes closed, head buried in his neck,

pressed close, savoring the solidity of his body, the security of his arms, the addictive smell of his skin, keeping tabs on her reactions.

So far really great.

Guest room? Who was she kidding? That wasn't like her at all, rationalizing and intellectualizing her feelings. She wanted him. He wanted her. It should be just that simple, always that simple.

Ames moved first, pressing kisses against her hair, on her temple, her cheek. Eva closed her eyes, gradually turned her face up to meet his mouth, keeping her thoughts away from feelings and analyses, indulging only the physical experience. Just in case the wobblies returned.

His lips took hers; she moaned in relief and pleasure. Yes. Yes. This was right, this was what she'd been wanting and needing during the long days without him. And the way he was devouring her, she suspected he'd felt the same.

Powerful chemistry between them. More than she'd ever experienced. But that was all it was.

His kisses were varied, thrilling, never staged or self-conscious. His back was warm and solid, his buttocks firm and round under her fingers. She could stand here and touch and kiss him all night.

His leg pushed between hers; his arms swept her back possessively. *Mmm.* She moved rhythmically against his thigh. Her arousal took off, her breathing stuttered. Stand here and touch and kiss him all night? Um, no. Eva wanted it all.

Impatiently she slid her fingers down to explore his erection, then gave in to temptation and sagged to her knees.

He had one of the most beautiful cocks she'd ever seen,

thick without being monstrous, pale with a blushing tip, smooth and the perfect length to take into her mouth without feeling she wasn't going to be able to handle it. He tasted clean from the shower, his skin soft and smooth.

His hands landed on her shoulders. He moved his hips gently, letting her control the depth, emitting a breathy groan when her hand found his testicles and added new sensations.

She liked this guy. He was hot and fun and sweet. If she could maintain her feelings at that same level, this could be her best three-week fling ever.

As if he had heard her thoughts, he opened his eyes and caught her peeking at him. "I like the things we do together, Eva."

"Me, too."

"I hope it's okay."

She quirked an eyebrow. "Do I seem to be suffering?"

"No, but…" He reached down and drew her to her feet. "We'd agreed on only one night."

"We did. But…"

"But…" He slid his fingers into her hair, drew her face up for a kiss. "One night wasn't enough."

"No."

He bent down; she responded instinctively with a small jump into his arms, and he carried her into the guest room and laid her down gently on the queen-size bed.

"Eva, I think I was wrong." He put his hands on his hips, looking down at her with concern.

"About?"

"About not wanting to see you as much as possible the entire time you're here."

"Ah." She smiled warmly, letting loose an internal shriek of victory. "It's a big man who can admit he's wrong."

"Yeah, you know…" He glanced down. "I'm feeling really *quite* big right now."

"I noticed that." She beckoned him up flush against the mattress, leaning forward to take him back into her mouth.

"Wait." He climbed onto the bed and turned so he could taste her at the same time.

Ooh, good idea. His mouth was skilled, his tongue very talented exploring her. He knew just where to put the pressure and how to vary the rhythm and speed of stimulation.

As her arousal increased, Eva took his cock in deeper, swirling her tongue, moaning at the pleasure he was giving her.

Did she mention she really liked this guy?

He moved away from her greedy mouth and turned to lie over her, kissed her hungrily, nudging her legs apart.

"Ames…"

"Mmm."

"Condom."

His face registered shock. "Right. Sorry. I was a little…carried away. Got out of the habit."

"You didn't use them with your last girlfriend?"

"Uh…no. She was on the pill. And I really don't want to talk about her with you lying there, naked and wet and—"

"Mmph." She clapped her hand over her mouth, then spread her fingers. "Yes, sorry. Bad sexual manners."

"I'll get one." He kissed her, slid out of bed and left the room.

Eva lay waiting, stretching her arms up toward the ceiling, feeling as though she'd won the lottery. Best of all, she wasn't feeling wobbly anymore. She was still crazy about Ames, but with the evening's trauma receding, her feelings were familiar again, fizzy and fun. She and Ames were supremely hot for each other and that was a good thing, a healthy thing, and would make the next three weeks really, really fun.

He was back in seconds with a fistful of condoms.

"Well." Eva started giggling. "I guess we're going to be busy tonight."

"You have other plans?"

"I thought I was supposed to get *more* sleep by staying here."

"You were." He sat on the edge of the bed and drew his hand down her body. "But that was before I saw you with your hair down, wearing nothing but a towel. And then not even that."

"That tipped it, huh."

"Yes, but I wanted you before that, Eva." He rolled on a condom, then bent over her, kissed her forehead, her nose, her mouth, her throat and down to take her breast into his warm mouth.

Breath whooshed out of Eva's lungs. "Oh, that is… really good."

"Mmm." His tongue circled her nipple; his teeth bit gently, causing a pain-pleasure response she felt all the way down between her legs. "I agree."

Eva was one lucky woman. She wouldn't be here right now, experiencing these exquisite sensations in her body and in her awareness of his, if she hadn't showered at the same time Ames did. If she hadn't called him earlier tonight. If Drunk Creepy Guy hadn't bothered her…

She should send him a thank-you note.

Ames began his adoration of her other breast, her other nipple…

Eva rolled to her side and hooked her leg over the top of his hip so his warm penis teased her sex, slight nudges that would take him where he wanted to go—where she wanted him, too.

He groaned and took hold of her buttock, pressing her firmly against his erection. "I'm getting this…this vision of our future."

"Yes?" She wriggled down slightly to improve the angle between their bodies. "Wait…I'm seeing it, too. It involves you deep inside me. Yes?"

"Yes." He rolled her to her back, grinning sensually, and kissed her. "Ye-e-e-es."

"Mmm." Eva reached for his erection with one hand and guided it home, spreading her labia with the other so he could slide in easily. "Ohhh." She spoke against his mouth, loving that first penetration, the way his cock gradually advanced, stretching her, pushing in, pulling out, bit by bit farther in until he filled her completely.

Ames gave a groan of pleasure, then lifted his head and met her gaze, somber and sweet. She felt breathless, almost dizzy, trying to smile, not sure why it was suddenly difficult. He started to move, sending jolts of sexual energy through her nerve endings, his eyes warm and tender holding hers.

Eva's almost-smile faded. Her heart gave a few uncertain flips. The wobbly feeling was back, as if she were on the brink of a chasm she didn't understand, wasn't sure she could handle falling into. She hooked her feet over his calves, used the leverage to return his thrusts, increasing the speed, trying to regain her stability in a solid base of desire.

It sort of worked. She closed her eyes, concentrated on the delicious friction of his erection inside her, the tugs on her clitoris that would eventually send her into ecstasy, the warmth of his chest against her breasts, the feel of his back muscles under her fingers, the bunch and release of his buttock muscles as he pushed in and out.

Sort of worked... Lifting her knees, she spread them wide, tightening her channel around him. Ames's breathing accelerated, became harsh. He slowed his movements, trying to hold back for her, then reached between them, rubbing her clitoris as he thrust, holding his weight up on his left arm.

Eva's desire rose, hot and sharp, became tinged with welcome desperation. The more she felt in her body the less she could feel in her heart. She thrashed on the pillow, lifted her head, let it drop, moaning, slave to this man's fingers on her, the penetration bringing her closer and closer to her climax, inevitable now, burning toward her, low and away, then sweeping her up slow-motion to a height where it stretched nearly interminably before bursting into a peak.

She cried out at the dizzying explosion, clutching his arms as her muscles contracted around him.

Ames dropped fully back onto her, pushing hard, then stiffened, thrust once, twice, breathing out in a harsh groan as he came.

Oh, gosh. *Oh, my gosh.* She wasn't sure she'd ever come that hard in her life.

No, it wasn't that. She hadn't come that hard *with* someone, feeling nearly a part of him. Not ever before. Not even close.

Oh, gosh.

She clasped Ames's body to her, panting, feeling his skin, his breath, his warmth. Instead of the usual exhilarating rush of triumphant infatuation, there was a deep, gravely sweet ache in her chest.

This wasn't right. This was weird. She should be happy, for heaven's sake. Men made her happy! Being held in a man's arms was sheer bliss. This was not bliss. It was somber and intense and almost frightening.

And when Ames lifted his head and gazed into her eyes without a hint of a grin, without a hint of the *score!* mentality, just a visual reflection of the lovely serious feeling inside her, it all became much worse. She nearly burst into tears.

Ames Cooke was so beautiful.

Eva Meyer was *so* messed up.

He excused himself to clean up. Eva lay still, staring blankly at the ceiling, giving herself a good talking-to. Something was troubling her, that was all. Maybe she was homesick for California and investing too much in her emotions around Ames as some kind of substitute safe harbor. Maybe deep down she felt guilty, that she should be home with Zac. Maybe she'd acted recklessly moving here, and didn't belong in this intense black-and-white city with all her crazy California colors.

No, no, that was all too dramatic, even for her. She had simply succumbed to fatigue and tonight's earlier drama. A good night's sleep and she'd be fine. In the meantime, footsteps told her Ames was coming back, and he was *not* going to find her mopey and confused after they'd had so much fun.

"Hey." Ames slid back into bed. "I enjoyed that, Eva. Maybe you could tell?"

She giggled at his blissful expression. "Uh, I had some idea, yes. Maybe you could tell I enjoyed it too when I came and my head nearly shot off?"

"Amazing."

"I know!"

He slid his arms around her. Miraculously, they found a comfortable position nearly right away. The extra arm that always got in the way didn't seem to be a problem.

Eva burrowed into him, prepared to lie in the unfamiliar embrace and count sheep.

She made it to about fifteen…and then…

Good morning.

Eva dragged herself up from sleep. Deep male voice, someone kissing her shoulder. Mmm, what a nice way to wake—

Wait, *morning?* Her eyes shot open. "What time is it?"

"Way early. You've got time to shower and get to the shop by five."

"Oh, my God, I can't believe I didn't set an alarm or anything." She threw off the covers. "You saved my butt."

"I set an alarm." His mouth was investigating her shoulder. "It went off in my room."

"I didn't hear it!" She tried to get up, but there was an iron arm around her waist. "Um. Ames?"

"Five minutes." His hand slid up to cover her breasts.

"No, no, there isn't time to—"

"Three minutes." He began pressing rhythmically against her bottom.

She giggled. "Why do they make men so horny first thing in the morning?"

"Because that's when they're likely to have women in bed with them."

"We're also there at night."

"Men are horny then, too. Doubles the chance for babies. Survival of the species."

"I'm more concerned right now about survival of the coffee shop."

"Aw, sure." He loosened his arm. "Abandon me in my time of need."

"Don't worry." She got out of bed and kissed his temple. "For the next three weeks I will make it my personal mission to help you out of as many horny moments as I can."

Ames grinned, holding out his arms. "My angel of mercy."

She snorted. "Get some sleep. I'll let myself out."

In the bathroom she showered superspeed, threw her hair into a ponytail on top of her head, dressed and brushed her teeth. On her way out, she stopped. Hesitated. Then backtracked, giving in to one last impulse.

Feet making no sound on the deep carpet, she tiptoed back to the guest room, dimly lit by the light she'd turned on in the hall, and peeked around the door. Ames was sleeping on his back, covers pushed down around his waist, broad chest exposed. Under the blankets, the shape of his muscular legs.

Eva's man for the next three weeks, to lust, honor and ravage, till California did them part.

Her lips curved in a smile. She'd been right: she felt much better this morning after a good sleep. Back on track, solid, consumed with thoughts of the café and what needed doing that morning and beyond. Today she wanted to think about inexpensive ways to change the feel of the shop, introduce softness, color and whimsy. She wanted to set up a date between Tom and Natalie. She wanted to find ways to—

"Have dinner with me tomorrow night?"

Eva jumped at the sound of his deep voice breaking the silence. Her smile grew wider. She wanted to find ways to enjoy this gorgeous man however possible while she was here.

"Thank you, Ames. I'd love that."

9

Eva wiped down the counter in front of the gleaming Beast one more time. After two weeks she still hadn't established a karmic connection with this machine. Back in California she had a sixth sense for hers, understood when it was feeling grumpy from too much humidity or heat. This one, she had to pull several shots each morning before she got it right, tasting each cup carefully, adjusting the grind, the dosing, the timing, sometimes fussing with the blend for maximum flavor balance, sometimes several times.

Besides that, so far the day had gone well. An October pumpkin-bread special had sold out—the rush of morning commuters had seemed particularly hungry—then they'd suffered the usual dead space midmorning. With lunch hour winding down now, the midafternoon lull had started. At the moment the store held Tom, in his jeans and sweatshirt as he was pretty much every afternoon, and an older man reading the *New Yorker*.

Those empty hours were the ones Eva wanted to target with her changes to the store. Commuters racing in and out didn't care about atmosphere; they wanted a quick jolt of caffeine, thanks, goodbye. But those who had the time and would rather linger—they needed luring in and they needed a reason to stay. For that reason, instead of cleaning for the two o'clock shift change, she was getting ready to close.

This afternoon she was conducting a grand tour of thrift stores with Ames. He didn't know that yet, but he'd find out soon. A quick call yesterday to Jean, always happy to snoop in the name of matchmaking, confirmed that Ames had only one appointment this afternoon, with a client he often complained needed more hand-holding than necessary. Further meddling—on Jean's initiative, Eva would never go that far—revealed that the client would be just as happy seeing Ames the next morning, in fact, the reschedule was really a better time. And voilà, Ames was free.

Jean was brilliant. Eva should give her a lifelong gift certificate to NYEspresso.

As for the shopping, Eva still hadn't made any firm decisions. She was counting on inspiration to determine what the narrow cold space needed to cozy it up. So far she'd come up with a few fun themes, but they made her nervous. Too much change could be jarring and disconcerting to customers. Natalie the decorator might have good ideas, but she'd either been crabby or rushing to go out whenever Eva fished for suggestions, and had responded only with grunts and promises to think about it.

"So what are we closing for, exactly?" Ben was working the register today. Rebecca's incessant chatter had made Eva thoughtfully share her with Jinx's time on bar. Ben was a little dense, maybe, a little rumpled, but a sweetheart, with tattoos and piercings that made Eva look like a rank amateur.

"I talked to Chris last night. I've been thinking the decor here could use a little changing."

"Yeah?" Ben glanced around dubiously. "Looks okay to me."

This from a guy who clearly didn't bother with a mirror in the morning.

"I wonder if it could be more…" Eva gestured around her. "Fun."

He looked skeptical. "Like fun how?"

"I don't know. Where do you have fun?"

"Bars. Baseball stadiums. Video arcades. Rock concerts."

"Ah." Eva drummed her fingers on the counter. "Not quite what I was thinking. More like the beach, or the zoo, or…"

"Like *kid* fun?" He was looking at her as if she was nuts.

Maybe she was. Eva felt herself reddening. "No, huh?"

"I'm not seeing it." He nodded past her, indicating a customer. "Yo, Tom."

Eva turned to find Tom at the counter holding his mug for a refill. "Another coffee?"

"Please."

"So what do *you* think of changing the decor here? Something a little more welcoming, maybe a little creative whimsy?"

"Uh." He scanned the store's interior. "Like…what?"

Eva sighed and handed him his refilled cup. Maybe this was a dumb idea. Or just dumb to ask men about it. Though Ames had seemed enthusiastic about brainstorming with her when she'd tried the previous night. Of course his ideas had been more like lining the walls with sex toys or pictures of her naked.

Such a help. But also such a sweetheart. They'd had more than one fabulous date this past week. Eva had worked hard to keep things light and playful between them, and so far so good. She was really enjoying him.

And what an awesome beastie in bed.

The door opened. Natalie strode in, looking model perfect as usual in a soft brown zippered jacket, a scarf in jewel tones that set off her dark coloring and black leggings tucked into brown ankle boots that showcased her membership in the mile-high-legs club.

Tom made a strangled sound and backed away from the counter, stumbled over a stool and barely managed to keep from spilling his coffee.

"Hey, Eva."

"Hey, Natalie." Eva winked at Tom. "What'll you have?"

"A red eye." She glanced behind her, noticed Tom, who waved lamely, turning bright red. "Hi, Tom."

"Hey." He seemed thrilled she remembered him. "How's it going?"

"Good." She glanced past him at his laptop. "Working?"

"Yes."

"On what?"

"A new piece. A concerto."

"For?"

"Harmonica."

"For *harmonica?* Three movements? Full orchestra?" Her eyebrows flew up in surprise when he nodded. "That is seriously weird."

"Thanks." He grinned proudly. "I even know a harmonica player who can pull it off."

"Ha!" Natalie handed Ben her money. "I'll have to hear that to believe it."

"Tom will invite you to the world premiere." Eva pulled Natalie's espresso, beaming maternally at them both.

Tom rolled his yes. "Yeah, that might be a while."

"You never know." Eva poured the shot into a cup of

coffee and handed it to her roommate. "Hey, Natalie, you have some time now? I thought we could brainstorm ideas for the shop."

"Oh." Natalie twisted her lip, consulting her watch. Eva sneaked a meaningful look at Tom, who stiffened in panic. "I could spare a few minutes."

"Tom, okay if we join you?" Eva pointed to Tom's table. This was too perfect. He and Natalie could get to know each other and fall madly in love in Natalie's few minutes. "You're here every day. You should be part of this."

"Sure. Yes. Okay." He rushed anxiously to clear the space of his books and laptop.

Natalie brought over her red eye and chose a chair. Tom sat next to her, looking as if he were about to have a seizure.

"So." Eva sat opposite Tom, hoping she could get them talking so she could leave them alone and finish cleaning to get out of here ASAP. "I'm thinking first of all, the place needs more color."

"You're sure Chris is okay with you making changes?" Natalie unzipped her jacket and unwound her scarf, somehow making the simple movements look wildly sensual. Tom's eyes were barely staying in his head.

"Yes, of course. I talked to her last night. I think the place needs to look a little more unexpected, a little more quirky and a little less—"

"Like Chris." Natalie spoke matter-of-factly. "And a little more like you."

"Ack." Eva clutched her chest. "I would not say that."

"But that's what you *are* saying."

"I think…" Tom looked back and forth between the women. "Right now the place is Schoenberg, and you want it more Mozart."

Eva blinked at him. "Uh. I do?"

"Ha." Natalie gave Tom an admiring look. "Clever."

"What is he talking about?"

Natalie lifted her chin, tipping her head so her auburn hair swung over one shoulder. She looked insanely beautiful. It was a little sickening. "Right now it's Thelonious Monk. You want Duke Ellington."

Eva stopped trying to understand.

"Donizetti instead of Strauss."

"Gershwin instead of Barber."

"I've got tickets to Norah Jones next week."

"Say *what?*" Natalie's head whipped upright so fast Eva was surprised she didn't injure herself. "You *do?* How did you score those?"

Tom shrugged. "I have my ways."

"Oh, my God, I *love* Norah! I would *kill* to go. You are so lucky."

Tom nodded. Cleared his throat. Nodded again.

Eva sat at attention. Was he working up the nerve to ask her?

Come on, Tom.

"So." He scratched his neck, turning bright red. "You want to go?"

Natalie's perfect jaw dropped. "You have an *extra* ticket for Norah Jones?"

"Uh. Yeah."

Natalie looked at Eva, as if to say, *Can you believe this?* "Wow."

"So do you want to go?" A hint of irritation. Poor guy was a nervous wreck.

"Are you kidding? I would *love* to."

"Yeah?" A grin spread across his face. He looked adorable. "Cool."

"You getting a group together? How many tickets did you get?"

His smile froze. "Just...two."

"Oh." Natalie was clearly taken aback. "So it's you and me going?"

"Yeah." Tom cleared his throat, pulled at his collar. "Should be a great concert."

"Well, yes." Natalie was eyeing him suspiciously. "Yes, it should be."

Silence.

"Uh, so, Eva." Tom fidgeted in his chair. "Back to your—"

"Yes, Eva." Natalie whirled back around. "The shop."

"Right." Eva jumped on her cue. "I was thinking of a more playful atmosphere, more inviting, maybe a theme, like beach or jungle or toy store or—"

"No, I don't think you want to go that far." Natalie had apparently recovered. "Soften the edges maybe, add color, maybe, but not go crazy."

"I agree. But Eva, you're right, the place needs something," Tom said. "I come here because it's close to my apartment. But it's not what I'd call homey."

"What do you have at home that you'd like here?" Eva asked him.

"Oh...I guess, neon lighting and 24/7 access to large-screen video games and porn."

The women stared in horror.

"Uh." Tom cracked a smile. "I'm kidding."

Natalie and Eva burst into laughter.

"And you believed me." He shook his head mournfully, clearly eating up the attention.

"Sorry." Natalie touched his arm, making him blush again. "But I do know people like that."

"We all do." Eva sneaked an encouraging wink at Tom.

This was going fine! She was so proud of him. She hardly had to do anything!

The shop door opened. Eva turned and gave a shout of pleasure. "Ames!"

He strode to their table, grinning, rain glistening in his hair and on his jacket. "I had a break, thought I'd come get a cup of my favorite coffee. Hi, Tom. Hey, Natalie. Eva, why is the store—"

"Hello there, stranger. Haven't seen you for a while." Natalie plunked her elbow on the table, rested her chin on her hand. She might as well have been saying, *By the way, I'm totally naked under my clothes, want to see me prove it?*

A good part of Eva's joy turned sour. "You know each other?"

"Sure." Natalie winked at Ames.

Eva had never socked someone in the nose before, but she could totally see herself doing it right now. Natalie had slept with half the city—why not the half containing Ames?

"We've bumped into each other here once or twice." Ames sounded politely amused. "I think you made fun of me for bringing Chris a box of pastries she'd just added to her own lineup."

"Mercilessly, as I remember." Natalie gave a sexy, satisfied smile. Her voice was lower, dripping sensuality. It was as if she'd turned into a completely different person. An icky one. No wonder she attracted men and then repelled them. She was faking it. "You totally deserved being taunted, Ames."

Eva gritted her teeth. She rarely gritted her teeth over people's behavior, but they needed gritting right now. She sneaked a look at Tom, whose jaw was tight enough to assume he was gritting right along with her.

"I probably did deserve it." Ames pulled up a chair between Natalie and Eva.

Natalie made a show of moving back her chair to make room for him, then yanked it closer after he sat down.

Come to think of it, Eva had never growled at anyone before, either, but...

Well, she was having all kinds of new and unpleasant impulses today, wasn't she?

"So what are you up to these days, Ames?" Natalie angled her body toward him. "Business going well?"

"Pretty good. A new restaurant here and there, fabulous menus to try. Trips abroad to sample excellent new wines." He whacked his forehead in despair. "Will it never stop?"

Natalie giggled archly. "You are fun. I had no idea."

Ames sent Eva a warm smile and put his arm around her. "That's because I only turned fun recently."

Natalie looked back and forth between them, clearly astounded. "So this is why Chris hasn't been complaining that you followed her to California?"

"That's why." He rubbed Eva's back affectionately. "I'm still here."

"Well." Natalie turned to glance at Eva as if she'd never seen her before. "Congratulations."

Congratulations? Now Eva felt like sticking out her tongue. It was totally unlike her to be jealous like this, feel inadequate like this. She was a smart, successful businesswoman—attractive, friendly, fun to be with and...

Why was she even having to give herself this pep talk?

She looked back and forth between Natalie and Ames, and the answer hit her.

Because Natalie and Ames would make a natural and stunning couple. Because they matched, complemented each other, would turn heads wherever they went, have kids perfect enough to star in commercials. Natalie was all the reasons Ames had been pursuing Chris.

The heads turning when she and Ames walked by would be thinking, *What does he see in Miley Cyrus?*

"Well, I have to get going." Natalie glanced at her watch and rose gracefully. "I have a client meeting at three across town."

Tom shot to his feet. "It's pouring out. I have a car, I can drive you."

She checked the streaming shop window, then turned to him in amazement, all her sex kitten artifice gone. In Eva's opinion she was ten times more appealing. "Across town? You'd do that?"

"Why not?"

"No, I'm… I mean, that's fine, if you're sure. In fact, it would be really great." She looked curiously at him as if she couldn't understand how a guy could actually be nice to her. "Thank you, Tom."

They walked out, Tom opening the door to the shop for her, then turning back to give Eva and Ames a surreptitious thumbs-up.

Eva returned the gesture, then arched a brow proudly at Ames. "I did that. They're going to a concert together, too."

"Natalie and *Tom?*" Ames gaped at her. "Are you serious?"

Eva sent him the evil eye. "Why not?"

"Well, she's so… I mean, and he's so…" He looked supremely uncomfortable.

"Uh…" Eva pointed between herself and Ames. "What are you saying, exactly?"

"Nothing." He grinned and pulled her in for a kiss. "I just realized I'm not saying anything at all."

"You are a very smart man." She got to her feet and offered her hand. "So smart that you are going shopping with me for the rest of the afternoon, and then we're coming back to decorate the—"

"I wondered why you were closing. I can't, I'm sorry." He looked sincerely regretful. "I have a meeting at three-thirty."

"Why don't you check your calendar?" She smiled sweetly. "Maybe the meeting got rescheduled."

Ames stared suspiciously and dug out his cell.

Eva looked over at the wall and counted bricks. *Dum-dee-dum-dum.*

"Rescheduled." He folded his arms, glaring at her. "What did you do?"

"*Me?* Nothing. Not a thing. Except have a short conversation with Jean asking about your calendar this afternoon. What she did after that she did alone."

He sighed with exaggerated misery. "You realize what this means."

"You get to spend the afternoon with me instead of talking to annoying people?"

"Life is so unfair."

She grinned and volunteered him to help her and Ben close. Outside, the rain was letting up, though a chilly, damp wind blew leaves and the occasional crumpled paper or cup down the avenue.

Eva pulled out a list of thrift shops. "Let's do this thing."

Three hours later, they were back, pulling up in a loaded taxi outside the store.

"That was fabulous!" Totally energized by their success, Eva managed to beat Ames to paying the driver—not easy, he was a quick draw with his wallet. They emerged onto the curb.

Ames groaned, putting a hand to his back. "I'm exhausted."

"You need to work on your shopping muscles."

"I need to work on my food consumption. I'm starving."

"Me, too. But we did great!" They'd done more than great. They'd had just about the best time Eva had ever had with anyone. Laughing, teasing, coming up with many more bad ideas than good as they roamed through shops sizing up people's discards. Ames had finally convinced Eva to abandon her theme ideas, and they'd settled on buying whatever appealed and come back with a bounty.

A whimsical teapot in the shape of a camel, various board games, a painting of a graceful flamingo, inexpensive "silver" trays to hold bakery items, an A-frame sidewalk chalkboard for messages and daily specials, paper cutouts of various fresh fruits, and Eva's favorite, an assortment of topiaries in whimsical materials—a miniature tree of shining red ceramic cherries, silk ivy shaped in a spiral, butterflies, roses, all in varying heights and shapes.

Nothing that couldn't be changed back in an instant, but Eva was bursting with excitement.

They unloaded the goods onto the sidewalk—miraculously the rain had stopped, though dark skies warned the respite was only temporary.

Eva unlocked the shop and turned on a light in the back office, leaving the door partly open. They carted in their haul, piling it in the middle of the darkened room. "Can you see okay? I don't want to turn on the big lights. People will think we're open."

"Smart." He smiled, incredibly handsome in the dimness, his earring glinting in the low light. "It's actually great."

Eva nodded. She knew what he meant. There was a wonderful sense of intimacy, with the damp city still going through its motions outside the door, and their private, still world so peaceful in here.

But if she kept smiling at him like this, and he kept smiling at her like that, she was going to get wobbly again from all she was feeling.

Maybe she should turn on the lights…

"So where do you want things?" He looked around uncertainly. "I admit interior decorating isn't really my strength."

"Me neither. But that never stopped me." She moved into the center of the space. "Let's start with the bakery case."

They lined the bottom of the white shelves with the paper fruit cutouts, then instead of the geometric white porcelain Chris had chosen, loaded in the silver trays, lowest in front, those on pedestals to the back. The effect was exactly as Eva had hoped, elegant but not stuffy, the mismatched trays keeping the display from being perfect, the fruit underneath fun and colorful.

On the long wall facing the tables, they pounded in nails and hung the flamingo, the jungle flowers and the ocean view, then stepped back.

Eva was thrilled. "Beautiful! Like they belong here! I can't believe how great they look!"

"Mmm, yes."

She turned to Ames. He was not appreciating art; he was looking at her in that dark-eyed predatory way that signified he was imagining them naked and wrestling.

"Ames," she said primly.

"Yes, Eva."

"We need to get this done."

"Oh, I agree." He took a step toward her, put his hands at her waist. He still looked predatory, but now his eyes held amusement, and that softness that made her feel all softened and strange. "There's a lot we need to get done."

Eva fought a tiny swell of panic. She'd been doing so well for so long keeping this vulnerability under control. What was wrong with her now? "I mean we need to—"

"I know what you mean." He drew her up against him and kissed her. The rain chose that movie-worthy moment to increase torrentially, hurling itself against the door and front windows.

She was cut in two, half wanting to struggle, to regain her balance, retain her control. The other half wanted to lose itself in this feeling of surrender, of lust and growing sweetness, feelings she was starting to think were new to her, and entirely inconvenient. She was leaving soon. What was the point of falling in love for the very first time in her life with someone she couldn't have, and who had made it clear he didn't want someone like her for the long-term anyway?

His mouth was warm and possessive, urging her to passion. His hands roamed her back, then lower, covering her bottom, sliding under the waistband of her kelly-green leggings, then under her panties, exploring her skin. His mouth left hers to go adventuring down the side of her neck, which was probably her third favorite place to be kissed.

She put up one last doomed attempt at resistance. "So we aren't…going to put up…topiaries?"

He tipped her face up to his, watching her intently. "That's what you really want to be doing?"

"Um." Her gaze faltered. "Well, I mean, no, I don't, but…I'm just excited about…that is, we *should* get the—"

"Eva." His voice was low, husky and achingly gentle. "What are you afraid of?"

"Afraid? Me?" She tried to laugh carelessly. No luck.

"Eva…"

Okay, never mind. She owed this man honesty. "I don't know."

"Describe your feelings."

"Well, one minute all I want to do is drag you behind the counter and have you do everything you've ever dreamed of to me."

He blew out a breath, looking as if he was having to keep himself from doing exactly that. "And the next minute?"

"I want to run as far and fast as I can go."

"Ever felt this before with anyone?"

She closed her eyes, shook her head minutely, hardly able to breathe. Was she falling in love with him? Could he tell? Would he make some excuse to get away from her, like, *Gosh, sorry, Eva, I forgot I'm scheduled right now to blast off for another solar system?*

"Hmm, this sounds serious." He laid his palm on her forehead. "Yup. You've come down with a bad case."

"Oh, no." She forced a giggle. "I'm afraid to ask what I have."

"But wait, there's more." He touched her hair, done up in an off-center bun and decorated with feathers. "I have it, too."

Eva stared up at him. Was he saying… No, no, this was too bizarre, he must be teasing. "Is this horrible condition transmitted sexually?"

"It starts that way. Then it spreads emotionally."

She shuddered comically, her heart still pounding double time, half hoping he'd say exactly what he meant and half hoping, please, for sake of her own peace, that he wouldn't.

"But the good news—" his arms came around her; he kissed her again "—is that since we both have it, we don't need to worry."

"Whew." She wasn't so sure. This wasn't her plan. Not to fall for him like this, so intensely and with such an air of finality. Love for her had always been a fun and delicious game, transient and nonthreatening to her character and her freedom.

He kissed her again, long and lingering, then faster and hotter, until her body temperature rose to match. She'd worry later; she'd cope with this confusing conversation later. Right now they needed nice, clean, uncomplicated sex to put everything back into balance, to get them into familiar simple and primal territory.

She pulled his perfectly ironed light blue shirt out of his perfectly ironed khakis and unbuttoned it impatiently, yanked up his T-shirt to expose his chest and pressed kisses to the smooth skin, inhaling his scent, as always amazed how this very basic exchange of physical information was so arousing. She loved the way he smelled. She loved the texture of his skin, the way it felt, yielding and warm against her mouth. Her fingers found the bulge in his pants and undid his zipper to reach in, hungry for the taste and feel of him everywhere.

He interrupted her, stripping the shirt from her body, unhooking her bra, clearly as anxious for her skin as she'd been for his. They came together breast to chest, and together emitted a sigh of relief—the horrendous separation of the past several hours had finally been ended.

The respite didn't last long. Soon they were struggling to shed the rest of their clothes, giggling when things didn't go smoothly—a sock still hanging ridiculously from a toe, balance threatened by standing on one leg, the condom in his pocket needing to be sheepishly retrieved after a macho move of hurling his pants into the back office. She loved that he was able to laugh at the good, bad and ugly, not feel as if sex were a performance, a power play or a bid for ego stroking or attention.

He whispered her name, pulled her tightly to him, devouring her mouth. She moved her hips against him, pleasuring herself and stimulating his already steel-rod erection, savoring the feel of his body tightening, the response of his breath, the deep, soft noises he made, the way he touched and kissed her everywhere.

Then his hands were on her hips, turning her away from him. She understood, braced her hands on the end of the counter and arched her back, offering herself to him, glad for the early darkness of October and the thick rain clouds making the light too dim for passersby to notice what they were doing.

He was there behind her, a warm solid presence, stroking between her legs, making her shiver.

"Mmm, that is a beautiful spot…and here, too. And especially…here." His fingers slid inside her, the pressure and movement making her gasp. "You like that?"

"Oh, yes." She could barely get the words out. "Yes, I like that."

"Same here." His fingers withdrew. She heard the sounds of a condom going on, then he grasped her hips and his searching penis gave her a warm nudge.

Leaning forward, Eva lifted her bottom, reached down between her legs and guided him.

The nudge became a pressure, the pressure grew, then he sank slowly into her. She moaned at the feeling, her nerves coming alive.

Even with Ames behind her, he was no anonymous

figure in the near darkness. Eva was hyperaware of his every movement, his every breath. She knew his eyes were half-closed, his jaw held tight. She tuned in to his breathing so she'd know best how to pleasure him, clenching her muscles to squeeze him tighter, lifting or lowering her buttocks, pushing back against his thrusts harder, slower, faster.

His hands covered her breasts; he pinched and gently tugged her nipples, adding to her arousal.

Eva moaned again, reached down and rubbed her clitoris, the extra stimulation making her orgasm only a matter of time.

Sensing her urgency, Ames increased his pace, rocking her body with his thrusts, both of them making primal noises of pleasure.

Warmth flooded Eva's body.

She was going to come.

Her climax hit in a sharp burst that convulsed her muscles, making her gasp…then it tapered off and gathered again, grew into something much bigger, so big she reared back, crying out as if the oncoming wave was a physical thing frightening her.

The second orgasm hit and she went over, barely coherent, unaware of anything but the push of Ames's cock and the immense pleasure that had taken control of her body and brain. Over and over she cried out, until Ames grabbed her hips and pushed violently, shouting as he came into her, pulsing and rocking until he, too, finally came down.

Then silence, except for their hoarse breaths. Eva stayed bent over the counter, hair fallen over her face, her heart pounding. She'd never experienced anything that powerful, physically or emotionally. She didn't want it to end. She didn't want to come down to the reality of what it might signify.

But of course she had to. Ames's erection receded. The counter became uncomfortable against her body. They couldn't stand here naked in a deserted store forever.

"Eva." His husky, awed voice told her he'd felt what she had. He pulled out of her, turned her toward him, gathered her rapidly chilling body in his warm arms and kissed her with such tenderness that tears threatened. When he pulled back, his eyes were reflecting what she felt.

"This wasn't supposed to happen."

"No. No, it wasn't." She shook her head, clutching him to her as if she'd drown without him. "We were supposed to put up the topiaries."

He laughed briefly, stroked her cheek with the back of his hand. "I'm not talking about the topiaries."

"I know," she whispered. And then the tears couldn't stay back any longer.

"The truth is—" he looked stunned, his eyes wide and dark, his face so handsome "—Eva, I'm falling for you."

10

THERE WERE THINGS Chris had really come to like about her life—or rather, Eva's life—here in central California. Like how the coffee shop was open 7:00 a.m. to 7:00 p.m. instead of 6:00 a.m. to 9:00 p.m. And how when she'd scheduled herself to work second shift, as she had today, she could sleep as late as she wanted, then get up and go running outside. In late October. No fighting other people for treadmill space at the crowded gym—this was real running. With amazing scenery, wide-open spaces, fresh ocean air…

Then she could go home and eat breakfast outside in her backyard if it was warm enough. Even bundled up against fog or a mild chill, it felt like an exotic treat. She got her eggs from a farm stand, her bread from a local bakery and all the produce was incredible—fresh and local, not trucked three thousand miles. After breakfast she could check out the competition in the area, or check in with her suppliers or read up on the latest news in the coffee world. All without Natalie around hogging the bathroom or fussing over her wardrobe or fighting with a boyfriend or ex. No sirens, no yelling—the worst noise pollution so far were the lawn maintenance people obsessed with leaf blowers. Special place in you-know-where for them.

Right now she was on her way to the café to relieve Summer for the afternoon shift. She would work five hours—five hours!—and that was it for the day; she'd still have an evening to herself.

That's when the small-town California bliss soured a bit. She'd gone out to dinner or to listen to music a couple of times with members of her staff—Summer, Melinda and Dana. Chris had also become friendly with a middle-aged neighbor couple who adored Eva and who had invited her over for a backyard barbecue. She'd gone to a couple of movies by herself, had joined an exercise class, but she didn't feel busy enough. As for the wild fling she'd decided to have, so far Gus had been the only serious candidate. That had gone nowhere on their first date, and the second had yet to happen. Most men she might have been interested in were customers, and as much as she'd have liked to drag a few of them behind the counter, that kind of thing was a risky business practice. To put it mildly.

If she was going to do something appropriate for what happens in California stays in California, she'd better get going soon. She and Eva were due to switch back in another week and a half.

Chris wrinkled her nose. When they'd decided to do this, a month had seemed to be a perfect amount of time. She hadn't expected it to fly by this quickly. There was a lot about this place she would miss.

Slow Pour was about a quarter full, a few of the outside tables taken, and inside—still no Zac. He hadn't been around for the past week. She'd actually wondered about him, hoped he wasn't ill. He was annoying, but not evil. She wondered how he'd feel if he knew that Eva was all about Ames in New York. Eva and Zac had given each other blanket permission to go wherever their hearts took them until age thirty, but she'd always wondered if Zac was secretly in love with her sister and hurt by her affairs.

In that case, he was a wimp for not fighting harder to win her.

She pushed into the shop, loving the initial coffee-everywhere smell that met her nose, then bent down and pushed the rubber doorstop shaped like a wide-eyed kitten—really, Eva?—into place. Gorgeous air like this should be allowed everywhere.

"Hi, Chris." Summer beamed, her abnormally white teeth glistening. Chris had gotten used to Summer's warm enthusiasm for absolutely everything, and no longer wanted to dose her with something for it. At least most of the time.

"How's the day been?"

"Not bad, just shy of seventy-five transactions."

"Not bad." She nodded approvingly, thinking there should be more. A glance around had her itching to simplify, get rid of the silly and useless things for sale, put in more tables, create a more efficient space, one that would encourage more people to choose Slow Pour for their morning jolt, and that would show tourists driving through Carmia that this was the perfect spot to grab a quick cuppa and a bite and be on their way.

Chris took over for Summer and found herself quickly fidgeting for more to do. The same customers had been sitting in the same chairs drinking the same cups forever. Only a few new transactions. She played in the back for a while with a blend she'd been tinkering with, and got something close to the balance she was after. Good enough to try out on customers, anyway.

Back in the shop, she made a slow tour with a pad and pen, jotting down ideas. Now that Eva had made changes at NYEspresso, Chris could start thinking seriously about doing the same here. Maybe she'd close early one afternoon, as Eva had. Maybe take down some of the surfer-dude stuff and local art, expose more clear space on the walls and more of the windows in the storefront. Her theory was that people driving by now saw junk for sale and not happy people drinking excellent coffee.

She was craning her neck up at the menu, hung on a surfboard, thinking that at least was too much fun to disturb, when she heard someone come in the shop, and she turned, looking pleasantly expectant.

"Hey, Chris." Zac lumbered up to the counter, his blue eyes crinkling into a smile.

Her heart skipped a beat. Good lord, what was that about? "Hey, Zac."

She wanted to ask where he'd been, but was afraid that would make it sound as if she'd missed him. Which she certainly hadn't. She'd just…noticed he was gone, that's all. Apparently she'd gotten used to having him around.

"You been doing okay here?" He stood close. She took a step back, grateful at least for the counter between them.

"Sure, sure, we've been doing fine."

"I asked how *you* were doing. Or did we become queen while I was gone?"

She glared at him, safe behind her irritation. "Do you deliberately make up ways to harass me or does it come naturally?"

His grin was slow and easy. "Yes."

Chris rolled her eyes, appalled to feel color coming into her cheeks. "What'll you have?"

"Just coffee."

"I'm working on a new blend, want to try?" One thing she really liked about Zac—he knew his coffee. "Forty percent Colombian, roasted Full City, then the rest is split fifty-fifty, Mexican roasted French and Kenya roasted City."

"Sounds interesting." He didn't even blink at her use of vocabulary indicating the level of roast.

"I'll be right back." She went into the back office to scoop up grounds from the batch she'd been playing with into a paper cup. "Here, see how it smells to you."

He leaned forward and sniffed quickly, then inhaled long and slow. "Nice. I'll try a cup."

"Good." She put a clean filter in the dripper and wet it from the kettle kept at a temperature just under boiling. Then she dumped the water out and put grounds into the filter.

"Have you talked to your sister lately?"

"Sure." She poured carefully, moistening the coffee as evenly as possible. "We're in touch all the time."

"I miss her. How's she doing in New York?"

Chris glanced at him, then put the kettle down to wait for the coffee to preinfuse. He didn't look particularly distraught, but then maybe he was one of those stoic guys who never showed emotion. "Good."

"That's all you can tell me? Good?"

"What do you want to know?"

"Is she happy there?"

"Yes. She's loving it."

"Is she getting out much?"

"It's New York—are you kidding me?"

"She dating anyone?"

Damn. That was the one question she didn't want him to ask.

"Oh, well, I mean…" She picked up the kettle again, started pouring slowly in a circle, pretending to concentrate so hard that she couldn't say any more.

"I'm not surprised. What's he like? Do you know him?"

"Zac..." She put the kettle down again. "I'm not really comfortable talking about this with you."

"Why?"

"Because I don't know what she'd want to keep private."

He looked at her as if she'd grown horns. "Eva and I have, like, zero secrets from each other. If she's found someone, I'm happy for her."

"Really?" Chris stared at him curiously. This was the reaction of a man who could be planning to marry her sister someday?

"Yes, really. Why would I lie about that?"

"I...guess I thought you had feelings for her."

"Chris." He leaned in. Up that close, his blue eyes were mesmerizing. "Do I strike you as the kind of guy who would be okay letting a woman I had deep romantic feelings for run off to New York and screw whomever she wanted?"

Chris should check the coffee to see if it had finished dripping and needed another pour, but she could not take her eyes away from Zac's. She was pretty sure they had been glued there. She wasn't even that sure what he'd just said. Something about having feelings for Eva. Or no, something else. She broke their gaze, hit mental rewind and paid attention that time. "How would I know what kind of guy you are?"

"If you stick around, Chris, you might find out."

She poured the second round of water over the grounds, more flustered than she wanted to admit, even to herself. "I'm leaving in a week and a half."

"You don't have to."

"Of *course* I have to. I have a life to go back to."

"Yeah?"

She was exasperated with him all over again. "Yeah."

"What about Eva? If she's having fun with someone, she might not be ready to come back here."

"That's ridiculous."

"Why? Have you talked to her about it?"

"No." She was getting upset, which was completely stupid, because there was absolutely no reason for her to be. Zac was just being his same creepy self and putting pressure on her for some bizarre reason. Because he wanted her to find out what kind of guy he was? So she should change her life plans? The ego! Jeez! Give her a break.

Besides, she owed creepy guys less than nothing, so she shouldn't even be *listening.*

"Coffee's ready." She handed him the cup, which she thought was pretty darn nice of her since she wanted to pour its contents down his pants.

A step back while she threw away the filter and grounds and took deep breaths.

Okay. Okay. She was fine now. Totally fine. She wasn't going to stay longer—Zac had just been asking, and everything was okay.

"This is excellent coffee." He took another sip, clearly savoring it the way an expert would. "Perfect balance, just the right acidity. Nice bite."

"Thank you." Chris couldn't help smiling. She was proud of her ability. Eva had a great palate, but she preferred the business and customer side of the trade. Chris was like their father—a serious coffee geek. Apparently so was Zac.

"Think about it."

He'd lost her. "About what?"

"Asking your sister if she wants to stay in New York longer."

"Don't you want her back?"

"Sure. But you need to be in California."

She bristled. "What does *that* mean?"

"Like roasting a bean darker to smooth down the acidity." His grin took away the offense, but Chris resorted to outrage anyway. Safer when he was being so intense, so close, and she was feeling so weirdly off balance around him. Yet again. "Like making sure you don't overextract an espresso."

"So you're saying I'm harsh?" She scowled at him. *"Bitter?"*

"And quite honestly—" his smile became devilish, his eyes warmed "—I want to get to know you better."

Chris took in a breath that didn't seem to want to come back out. "Because you might marry my sister someday."

"Hmm." His eyebrow quirked. "What do you think?"

"I think you are messing with me." She stepped back from the counter, turned away from his magnetic presence with the excuse of refilling the kettle and setting it back on the burner.

The most annoying man on earth. Thank goodness she was getting out of this place in less than two weeks.

An odd darkness settled in her stomach at the notion. And it bothered her that she'd thought of leaving as an escape, as if she was running away more than returning to where she belonged.

"Yo, Chris. How's it going? Hey, Zac, my man!" The sound of Gus's voice was predictably followed by the slap of a high five.

Chris turned, smiling, grateful for the interruption. Gus was *so…*Gus.

"Hey, there." She was glad Zac had stepped back from

the counter, giving her a little more room to breathe again. Or maybe it was Gus who'd brought the air back into the shop. He was looking wildly sexy as usual in shorts and a T-shirt, dark hair curling and still wet from the surf. "How was the competition?"

"I am the man!" He lifted both arms over his head, face glowing. "Third place!"

"Nice job!" Chris applauded.

"Way to go." Zac lifted his hand. *Slap*. These guys needed something else to do with themselves.

"Thanks. I'm stoked. Next time I'll do better. I need to land a sponsor."

"Coffee and treats on the house." She gestured to the glass case. "What do you want, Gus?"

"No caffeine." He shook his head, scattering droplets, and shoved his hair back with his hands. "I'm into natural highs from sunshine and waves."

"Juice? Muffin? Cookie?"

"Organic? Sugar-free? Whole grain?"

Chris cracked up. "Okay, okay. I'd offer you a Slow Pour T-shirt, but I can't fill you in on factory conditions or worker wages…"

"Glass of water would be good." He turned behind him, searching. "My friend and most fabulous mentor Bodie Banks is coming any second. He had to stop in for more sunscreen."

"Bodie's here?" Zac was smiling approval. "It will be good to see him."

Bodie and Gus. They sounded more like ranch hands than surfers. "So what's next for you, Gus?"

"Yeah, so listen, Chris." He glanced uneasily at Zac and stepped up close to the counter. Immediately, Zac took the hint and went back to his table. "I totally owe you dinner." Gus's eyes were dark and earnest, and so beautiful it was like having her own personal movie star. Even better, the eyes didn't make her feel as though her identity was dissolving. They were just really hot. Though this close—he suddenly looked so boyish. She'd placed him around twenty-five, just a couple of years younger, but… "Just you and me. Inside, in a restaurant. Some place romantic. I swear I won't go near a surfboard the whole evening."

"Before I answer, one question." She grinned at him. "How old are you?"

"Aw, come on." He stepped away from the counter in disgust.

"What?" She giggled. "How old?"

"Younger than you think."

"Fourteen? Fifteen?"

He snorted dismissively. "Yeah, right. I'm twenty-three. I will be soon, I mean."

"You're *twenty-two?*"

Zac looked up. Smirking.

Good God. She'd practically be a cougar.

"But I'm… I mean, it's not like we're going to get married, right?"

"You're right." She looked up into those movie-star eyes and smiled, still able to see Zac's smirk in her peripheral vision. So Gus didn't mind older women, huh? She wasn't sure how she felt about the age difference. But she was sure about one thing. It would hurt no one to have dinner with the kid and see what happened.

"I'd love to have dinner with you, Gus."

"Awesome!" He lifted his hand for a high five. She didn't move.

"Hey, this is the place." The deep voice came from the entrance, behind Gus.

"Bodie!" Zac turned, this time with his hand up confidently. *Slap.*

Coming into the shop was the sexiest man Chris had ever seen—besides Gus. And Zac.

Bodie was powerfully built, in his thirties, with one of those craggy ultramasculine faces that wasn't necessarily handsome but didn't need to be. A Daniel Craig or Clive Owen face.

His eyes met hers, and he stopped in the entrance to the shop, hands on his hips, his friend Gus apparently forgotten, and stared at her with as much interest as she was staring at him.

It was suddenly difficult to breathe.

In her peripheral vision she saw Zac standing abruptly, closing his laptop.

Okay. Chris needed to think about this. She'd wanted to have some kind of wild adventure while she was here in California. Right now she was standing in her sister's coffee shop alone with three of the sexiest men alive, all of whom appeared to find her attractive, which had never, ever happened to her in New York or anywhere else in her whole entire life.

And she was planning to *leave?*

11

AMES PUSHED BACK the chair in his condo office. He was tired, frustrated by an afternoon of fruitless calling, and he missed Eva. Missed her! It was as if they were in a serious relationship instead of just having a fling.

Yeah, guess what.

He still wasn't sure how it had happened. He'd just been going along, enjoying her craziness, her color and her spirit. Then somewhere along the way part of her had sneaked inside him. Or maybe part of her had awakened the part of him that remembered how to enjoy itself. Either way, Ames had begun to change. He'd become impatient with the long hours he put into his job, the months of constant travel, the restrictive attitudes about how to look or behave. He'd started thinking about how much he missed playing basketball and baseball, how he'd like to start going to more concerts and plays—after all, he lived in the cultural center of the country, if not the world—speaking from a New Yorker's perspective, of course. He'd like to read more, and yeah, maybe relax a little.

Preferably with an exuberant, beautiful woman at his side. Naked some of the time. Or a lot of the time.

His past relationships seemed bland and shallow next to this vibrant, exciting woman who'd taken one look and realized what Ames had lost and how he could get it back. Who'd taken on that job with a determination that never veered over the line into an attempt to control him. His infatuation with Chris seemed so middle school now, his determination to win her arrogant and shortsighted, more about his own ego than who she was or what they could bring to each other.

And yet…he and Eva had been having fun in a bubble. He hadn't met her friends, and she hadn't met his, or interacted with his colleagues. The Boyce client dinner was a week and a half away, the Saturday before she went back to California, and he had yet to answer battle-ax Delores's increasingly annoyed emails and calls as to whether he was bringing a date.

Ames still had to get over or come to terms with his issues about Eva's appearance. He also still had to come to terms with being someone who cared that much about appearance. He wasn't sure he liked that about himself.

Round and round and round he goes, where he—

"You've got chicken gumbo on the stove, and I am gone." Jean stared suspiciously into his office, working to control a smile. "What, daydreaming *again?* Whatsa matter with you—you in love or something? Get back to work!"

"Jean." He closed a client file and stood, drawing his hands down his face. "I'm closing shop."

"Already?" She stared at her enormous black watch. "It's only five. That's when *normal* people knock off."

"Maybe I'm getting normal."

She smirked at him. "Anyone coming over to keep you company tonight?"

"No." He acted surprised. "*Should* there be?"

Jean threw up her hands. "No, of course not. You should be alone every night with your balls shriveling and turning blue."

"Ooh." He cringed. "Thanks for that image."

"You call her right now and invite her over for gumbo or I swear you'll die alone. I'm outta here. You take care, Ames."

"Thanks, Jean. See you Thursday."

"Only if I live that long…" She stalked out of the office. A few seconds later, the front door closed behind her.

Ames walked into his living room. Then his bedroom. Then the kitchen.

Maybe he should call Eva.

He looked into the refrigerator, pulled out a beer, popped off the top and took a swig.

No. Nothing had been said, but he was pretty sure they both needed a night off after yesterday's intensity after hours at NYEspresso. Certainly he did. Today felt like some kind of crossroads. Either he had to decide he couldn't get serious with a woman who lived across the country and who wouldn't blend into the rarefied environments that were inevitably part of his life, or decide he could. Pull back or move forward.

Which?

Back in his living room, he gazed out at the terrace, perfect for hanging out on summer evenings, big enough for entertaining. He'd done very little of either, always on the road or sitting at his desk.

Where had those plans gone? When was the moment he'd been sucked in over his head for the job, both in amount of time and attitude? How had he let so much slip through his fingers? How much more of his life would he have missed out on if he hadn't met Eva?

Maybe he should call her.

He took another swig of beer, paralyzed by indecision.

No. No. Not tonight.

EVA LET HERSELF into her apartment. She was tired. Work had been exciting today; the changes to the decor had gotten lots of talk, at least. She thought maybe a few people had lingered longer than normal, but one day wasn't nearly enough to compile meaningful statistics.

After work, she'd wanted nothing more than to show up at Ames's condo with dinner or some other offering and distract him from whatever he was doing in a thoroughly naughty and fabulous manner.

But.

She was under the impression they both needed a break after yesterday. She sure did. Their relationship had been so easy and energizing when she'd been in the lead, dragging him around to play mini golf, shaking up his life, changing his routine, interrupting his shower....

Now she was the one shaken up and changing. Now her life plan was in danger of being interrupted.

"Yes! Oh, my God, I loved that show! She was amazing, wasn't she?" Natalie's voice emerged from her bedroom as Eva went past. A male voice mumbled unintelligibly on the other end. Eva glanced in to nod and say hi.

Oh, my gosh!

She stopped on the other side of the door, dying to backtrack and peek in again.

Natalie had been draped over her bed on her stomach, bare feet waving in the air, phone pressed to her ear, cheeks flushed, eyes shining.

And she was *smiling*.

"Sure, no problem. Yes, I'll see you tomorrow. Bye!" The sound of a phone dropping onto the bed. *"Hey, Eva! You can stop eavesdropping now."*

D'oh! Eva stepped back into view. "Sorry. Just being nosy."

"No kidding." Natalie frowned, trying unsuccessfully to look her usual sour self.

"Well, then." Eva folded her arms. "You might as well tell me who that was."

She shrugged and climbed off the bed. "Tom. We were making arrangements for tomorrow."

"Oh?"

Natalie narrowed her eyes. "What does that mean?"

"The Norah Jones concert's not until Friday…"

"So?"

"So nothing." Eva smiled sweetly. "See ya."

She pretended to move on, then peeked quickly into the room again. Natalie had thrown herself on the bed, on her back this time, and was staring dreamily up at the ceiling. Her face collapsed into a scowl and she covered her face with her hands. Then something made her giggle and she was back to dreamy again.

"Ha!"

Natalie shrieked. "Jeez, you nearly gave me a heart attack. What is your problem?"

"You like this guy." Eva pointed accusingly. "And you don't know what to do about it."

"What makes you think that?"

"He's not your *type*." She drew air quotes around the word. "Because he's no one you could ever see yourself getting serious about, and then he turns out to speak your language and be incredibly sweet and wonderful and you're completely turned upside down."

Natalie was looking at Eva as if she'd shed her human skin and was showing alien. "What have you been smoking?"

"Well?" Eva refused to buy the cold-bitch act this time. "Am I right?"

"Humph. Possibly." She couldn't hide a smile. "But I am taking the man to my salon, and then shopping for decent glasses and clothes. I am not going to be seen with him looking like...he looks."

Eva's turn to roll her eyes, while dismay jabbed her. That hit a little close to home. Though at least Ames had been seen in public with her several times and hadn't yet suggested she restyle her hair and shop at Brooks Brothers. "That is so deep!"

Natalie giggled. "Leave me alone. This is all your fault."

"I know. I'm *really* sorry I caused you any happiness." Natalie and Tom, score one for Eva! Her phone rang. She grinned and continued toward her bedroom to answer it.

"Hey, Chris. How's things going out in sunny California?"

"Great! I'm *loving* it here."

"Yeah?" She felt a little sick. Her sister better not be that high on anything having to do with Gus. "How did the second date with Gus go? Fabulous? Stupendous? He dazzled you with his intellect? He astounded you with his brilliant—"

"Stop. Now. Poor Gus. And no, our second date hasn't happened yet. He keeps coming up with excuses." She sounded exasperated. "I think I terrify him."

"I'm sure you do. You have a brain." Eva couldn't stop smiling. "So can I say it yet?"

"*No,* you can't say it."

"Aw, c'mon, I earned it."

"Okay, okay, you told me so. He is not a rocket scientist. But he is still absolutely delicious to look at. Now your turn—what's going on with Ames? Can *I* say it yet?"

"Nope. You can't."

"Really?" Chris gasped. "Well, but…you guys aren't actually *dating,* are you? I mean, you're just hanging around, right?"

She sounded so incredulous Eva burst out laughing. "Yes! We are dating!"

"I can't believe it."

"It's true. He's great."

"Jeez, never in a million years would I— Wait." Her voice grew suspicious. "Did he invite you to the big client dinner?"

A twinge. "No."

"Eva—"

"No, it's fine. I don't blame him, seriously. Can you see me there?" She forced a laugh. "Really, we're just having a great time playing and being goofy and, I don't know, just having fun."

"Goofy? Fun? Ames Cooke? Are you sure you have the right guy?"

"I'm sure, Chris." The words suddenly hit her in a different way, and they felt true and honest from deep down. Eva sat with a thump on the bed. This had started as another fun romp with a handsome guy, but it had turned on her. She had developed serious feelings for him.

Now what? If he was really falling for her, as he said, would he invite her to this dinner and all the others like it, or keep her hidden? Would he be like Natalie with Tom and try to turn her into what he really wanted?

"Eva?" Chris sounded worried. "You're acting weird. Are you okay? What's really happening?"

Eva stared at the wall opposite her bed, all of four feet away. She was suddenly terribly homesick for the relaxed, open spaces of California. She could breathe there. She was at peace.

"I think I'm falling in love with him."

MAYBE HE SHOULD call just to see how—

Ames's phone rang. He yanked the device out of his pocket so hard he nearly let go of it, which would have sent it halfway across the room.

It wasn't Eva. It was the battle-ax. He could not ignore her any longer.

"Well, hello, Ames. I'm so glad you remembered how to answer your phone."

He didn't bother making excuses. "I know. I owe you an RSVP."

"Really, take your time."

He sighed. A picture rose in his mind of the elegant white tablecloths in the private dining room at La Grenouille Laide, the space full of sleekly elegant couples—Mr. and Mrs. Boyce, some of their best customers, generally older and impeccably styled, the rest of the senior sales team and their dressed-for-success wives, Ames in a tuxedo and Eva, hair in seven or eight ponytails, wearing her usual joyous assortment of colors and styles, maybe those red high-top sneakers she'd worn on one of their dates.

He pictured himself there without her. The room looked darker without her. Plainer. The joy was gone, the company dull.

Then he pictured Eva sitting home alone, aware that he'd rejected her, and why.

My God, he was an ass.

"There will be two of us."

"*Thank* you." She sounded totally exasperated. "Does she have a name?"

"Eva Meyer." He gave a long, sappy sigh, giddy with

happiness, and suddenly wanting to stick it to Delores for being so unpleasant all these years he'd been with the company. "I'm in love with her, Delores. I think she might be the one."

Silence. Ames had to work not to crack up.

"She's incredible. I mean, *really* incredible, Delores. I've never met anyone like her. But she's not my usual type, you know? She dresses kind of crazy, piercings and tattoos and stuff, so I hesitated to invite her. But then today I thought, what the eff? I love her—who cares what those stuffy bastards think? Am I right, Delores?"

He waited, grinning. He'd gone completely off the deep end. Word would get to his boss and his boss would fire him. And guess what? Not having this job wouldn't be the end of his world.

"I think you are right, Ames, yes." Her voice had softened. She sniffed a few times. "My family thought I'd married beneath me. I've never regretted the time I had with William, not for a single day. I wish you all the happiness in the world."

Ames blinked, stunned and incredibly touched. How many more times would he judge people on first impressions and be proved wrong before he finally learned? "Thank you, Delores. Thank you very much."

He hung up the phone, feeling incredibly light. No more wasting time worrying about what his boss and colleagues thought about his choices. If they didn't like them, there were other jobs, other, younger companies that would be more liberal and accepting.

Eva had done to him what she'd been doing to NYEspresso—bringing in color and fun, getting rid of sharp edges and straight lines, celebrating a mixture of styles.

His gaze was drawn abruptly to one bare corner of his apartment. He knew what he had to do.

But first, he was going to call her.

EVA DRIFTED INTO the living room, walked around its perimeter, which didn't take long, and back into her bedroom. Did it again. Then flopped onto the bed with a groan of frustration.

Chris had not reacted well to her declaration. She didn't trust Ames, didn't think he was showing signs of taking Eva seriously enough, and had added the cheery note that if they decided to keep dating long-distance, he'd probably dump her for the first supermodel who showed interest. He was a type, and had been raised among people of that type and was programmed to settle down with that type eventually, even if he really enjoyed Eva's novelty in the meantime.

Yeah, well, Eva hadn't wanted to fall in love with Ames. She hadn't wanted to be in love with *anyone*. She wanted to grow comfortably old with Zac, who was the most lovely man on the planet but who never made her pale with fear and insecurity and vulnerability. Of course, he never made her tremble with passion, either, but she'd take that over being a basket case.

Love made you bipolar! Up and down, manic then depressed. She wanted to be steadily, lightly and happily carefree, not bogged down by angst. Look at her: she'd only just admitted to herself that she was falling in love, and she was more depressed than she'd been in years.

Her phone rang.

Adrenaline shot through her system. She bounded up from the bed and grabbed her cell.

Ames! A smile burst onto her face; she wanted to break into a jig.

See? Crazy! Up and down and up and down. Crazy and exhausting.

She considered not answering, but that was utterly impossible. She had to hear his voice.

"Hi, Ames."

"Eva."

She closed her eyes. His deep voice. Saying her name. Oh, man. "What's going on?"

"Just thinking about you."

"Nice thoughts?"

"Very. And I had two questions. One, I would really like you to go with me to the Boyce dinner next week."

Eva held her breath. He wanted her there! Even though she looked nothing like Natalie or Chris! Unless…oh, God. Was he about to bring up the salon visit and clothes-shopping trip?

"That's not a question."

His low chuckle thrilled her. At the same time, she was gripping the phone so hard her fingers were starting to hurt.

"Eva. Would you please come with me to dinner next week with all my stuffy and boring clients and colleagues and give me some hope of enjoying the evening with your spirit and beauty and insane hairstyles and hummingbird tattoo and wacky clothes on an amazing body that can make mine forget there are any other women in the world?"

Eva closed her eyes blissfully. *Oh, my.* What girl could resist that? He might dump her for a supermodel someday, but for now, he was accepting her, loving her exactly as she was. She could barely make her throat open enough to speak. "Yes. I would love to. Thank you, Ames."

He exhaled as if he'd been holding his breath, and she

decided if this next question was as complicated and over-wrought as the first one, she would probably explode.

"And second, Eva, I want you to eat chicken gumbo with me."

She made a dismissive noise. "That's not a question, either."

"Hey, you want to give me a break here?"

"Is *that* your question?" She was grinning now, having emerged from the emotional moment into another round of giddiness. They'd crossed another threshold together just now, an important one. Where this would take them was anyone's guess, but when had she done anything but dive in and find out?

"I'm trying to ask you to come over and spend the night with me."

"Okay." She did a stupid dance around the room, which took all of about four steps. "Go ahead."

"Go ahead what?"

"Well, duh, ask me the question." She probably wouldn't stop smiling for the rest of the night, already thinking of what clothes to bring and how fast she could throw them together.

"Eva."

"Mmm?"

"Would you like to come over and spend the night with me?"

"Wow, Ames, that *is* a question. You're right!"

His growl of annoyance was like an aphrodisiac. She couldn't find it in her to tease him anymore. Not when all she wanted was to rush over there as quickly as possible and into his bed.

"Yes, please, Ames. There's nothing else in the world I'd rather do."

12

EVA WIPED DOWN the counter after the latest batch of customers. Slowly but surely, midmorning and midafternoon business had been picking up. A few customers had come in asking about the specials listed on the sidewalk chalkboard. A few customers had even played some games, and with more tables filled it seemed like more people were comfortable stopping in. The Stay Mellow decaf options had been selling well. If Eva had more time here, she'd try out some of her herbal tea blends that had been popular at Slow Pour. And she'd look into nonprofit events coming up in the city and try to become a sponsor, to get NYEspresso's name out in public.

Right now the café was half-full, good for a Friday afternoon. Tom and Natalie were giggling like teenagers, engrossed in a fierce bout of Sorry! Eva couldn't believe the change in both of them. As Natalie threatened, Tom had been taken for a makeover, and while he'd never be George Clooney, he looked considerably less dorky—no, he actually looked quite handsome—in stylish clothes that matched and fit, and with a decent haircut and glasses that better fit the shape of his face.

Eva would be feeling queasier about him being taken in hand like that if Natalie hadn't also changed because of her romance with him. Outside of client appointments for which she still dressed to kill, Natalie had been wearing less makeup, letting her auburn hair dry to its natural curly state and throwing on comfortable sweaters over jeans. It was as if she didn't try so hard to impress, as if she felt more comfortable in herself, now that Tom was adoring her for herself instead of just what she looked like.

Eva had been thinking about that a lot. Tonight was the Boyce Wines dinner at La Grenouille Laide. A few weeks ago, every piece of her soul would have rebelled at the idea of catering to smug rich people by dressing in any way that didn't express who she was.

Now she was starting to wonder how much of her true self was really encapsulated in her clothing. Was dressing semioutrageously all that important? Did she have the right to cause ripples in Ames's world by making a loud statement all about herself? Couldn't she still be Eva Meyer while respecting the company she kept? By respecting Ames enough to play nice with people important to his future? For *one night?*

Heavy questions. She'd gone shopping the day before and found a little black dress, clingy and plain, but with a playful ruffle and bit of lace here and there, funky enough to suit her but still giving off the impression of cool sophistication. She'd put her hair up in a French twist and added a black fascinator with silver leaves and delicate feathers she'd pounced on in a vintage clothing shop. One set of earrings, one simple silver locket of her grandmother's around her neck.

The dress looked great on her. She should be proud to wear it as Ames's date, and she would be. But the odd thing was, now that she'd ensured she'd blend in with the crowd, the dinner party intimidated her even more. Which made her wonder if the way she dressed hadn't been so much an expression of her true self, her creativity and nonconformity, as a strong visual statement of who she wanted to be, something she could hide behind. Tonight, dressed like everyone else, she imagined she'd feel totally naked.

Right now she felt great. To offset the supreme sacrifice of planning to wear mainstream clothing, that morning she'd put on her zebra-striped tights and a rainbow polka-dot shirt over silver platform sandals. Her hair was arranged in a sloppy pile on her head, decorated with tiny clip-on stuffed animals, puppies and kittens and baby seals. Of her four pairs of earrings, two reached past her shoulders, and she'd counted out fifteen bracelets.

She might be conforming tonight, but when she showed up at Ames's apartment after work, he wouldn't forget that she was still going to be this kind of girl sometimes.

Four o'clock finally came—she didn't know if she'd been anticipating or dreading it more—and Eva was on her way. By the time she made it to Ames's building, she was, admittedly, a wreck. She wasn't much of a drinker, but it might not be a bad idea to have a shot of something before they arrived at the dinner. A fifth of courage.

"Hey, Frank." She beamed at the doorman.

"Well, don't you look colorful today? I'm cheered up just looking at you." His grin was sincere, and Eva smiled back warmly.

"Thanks, Frank." She still thought having a guard for a building was odd, and missed being able just to walk into friends' houses in California without all the security, but she liked Frank, and liked that she was expected and cleared through now, without having to bluff her way in or rely on Jean.

"He's expecting you."

"Thanks." She went into the elevator and punched the

button for the sixth floor, fidgeting. What if she said something awful tonight? What if she offended everyone every time she opened her mouth, and they sat in a circle around her pointing and laughing? What if they fired Ames and tied her up in the alley until she stopped—

Okay, okay. That was silly. But she was crazy nervous. She wanted to call Chris. She wanted to talk to Zac. She wanted to wander down to Aura Beach, sit in the sand and watch the sun set over the Pacific without a care in the world.

Easy. Safe.

Ames opened the door after her first knock. Frank must have called him after all. Or had he been waiting? He was probably nervous, too. Wondering if she'd chosen an outfit for the party that would fit on an avant-garde movie set.

"Hello." He grinned, eyes traveling up and down her crazy outfit before he drew her close and kissed her. "Running away to join the circus?"

"Oh, no!" She pretended dismay. "I picked this out for tonight—you don't like it?"

He kissed her again. "If you didn't have a garment bag over your shoulder, I'd be panicking."

"Wait until you see what's in *here!*" She held the bag up threateningly.

He lifted his hands. "Eva. I'm ready. Whatever you want to wear is fine with me. They will just have to get over themselves."

Oh, gosh. A guy like that could make her seriously crazy about him.

Wait, she already was.

"You—" she laid a hand on his cheek "—are wonderful."

"You—" he laid a hand on her bottom "—are hot."

"Hmm, maybe you think so." She pushed a finger into his chest. "But not nearly as hot as you are."

"Oh, yeah?" He was grinning, and she was grinning right back at him. The atmosphere was electric, as if they both had energy shooting out of their pores and filling the air. Two nervous people…

"Let's settle this." She hung the garment bag in his coat closet and turned to face him, grabbing the hem of her shirt. "Take off your clothes."

"Fine." He yanked off his T-shirt, exposing that chest that made her heat up like a radiator. "I will."

She unhooked her bra, threw it behind him. He kicked off his shoes, yanked off his socks.

She did the same.

They got out of their pants and underwear in record time and stood looking each other over critically, hands on their hips.

"No. No." Eva pointed to his torso. "See, you're hotter. Look at that—that is truly spectacular. Broad, muscular shoulders, flat stomach with superb definition—"

"Strong, slender arms." He pointed to her body. "Round breasts that make men want to weep. Narrow waist—"

"Fabulous ass."

He pointed lower. "Very sexy woman parts."

"Extremely erotic man parts."

"Nice legs."

"Nice legs."

Their arms lowered, they stood beaming like fools.

"It's a tie." Without warning, Eva took a running leap and launched herself at him. He caught her with a shout of laughter, staggering back into the living room, turning to keep his balance. He ended up losing it anyway, twisting to fall so he caught the brunt and she was on top of him, her hair a loose mess, animals scattered everywhere

Perfect. "Hello."

"Eva." He was slightly out of breath. "Do you ever do *anything* anyone expects you to?"

"Why, yes, Mr. Cooke." She wiggled suggestively, bracing her knees on the rug. "For example, I'm about to fulfill all your expectations right now."

"Ah. Well, that's good, actually. That's just fine."

"You're sure?" She stretched his wrists over his head and leaned on them to keep him immobile, teasing his rapidly hardening penis, loving the warm feel of it rubbing against her clitoris. "Are we allowed to do something this naughty before we mingle with the highbrow?"

"Oh. Yes." His eyes started bugging out a little as she continued to move.

"Do we have time?"

"Yes. We. Do." He moved up, his erection trying to find a way in. "Plenty. Lots. Tons. Really."

"Okay, then." She rocked back and forth, not letting him inside her yet. "Ames."

"Ungh." His caveman grunt made her smile.

"I'm nervous about tonight."

He opened his eyes, stared into hers briefly, then heaved his body and rolled them over so she was underneath, her wrists pinned over *her* head. "I'm nervous, too, Eva."

"Really?"

"Really." He began to move, rubbing his cock over her sex without entering—a taste of her own medicine.

Her own medicine was, frankly, fantastic.

"Nervous because of me and how I might act?"

"No." He stopped moving. "No, not that at all."

Something relaxed and sweetened inside her. "Okay."

"I'm nervous because if you don't have a good time I will feel responsible." He was looking down at her with deep tenderness; she nearly wanted to cry. "And I will feel terrible."

"Ames," she whispered.

"I don't want either of us to feel terrible." He began to move again, making her body leap back into arousal. "I want us always to feel as good as we do right now, naked and rubbing all over each other with possible heaven just around the corner."

Eva giggled. "Greedy."

"You think so?"

"I know so." She gathered her strength and twisted to one side, bucking him off, then used the momentum to push him the rest of the way onto his back so she could sit astride him. "I'm nervous because you delayed inviting me. Which is fine, I understand, but obviously this is a big deal and you had questions about how I would fit in. Frankly, so do I."

She held his beautiful brown gaze, wanting him to be straight with her, even if it was really hard.

"I did." He returned her gaze calmly. "I couldn't picture you there. I thought you'd be uncomfortable, but I also I thought I would be. I'm not proud of that now, but it's the truth."

She nodded, touched by his sincerity. "What changed?"

He smiled, pressing his hand briefly against her cheek. "I was focusing on the wrong thing. As hard as it was at the beginning to imagine us there together, I reached a place where I simply couldn't imagine going without you."

"Thank you." Tears threatened her eyes, clogged the back of her throat. Hadn't she told her sister she was falling in love with Ames? If falling was a process, this was the end point. She loved him. He was noble and sweet and willing to escort her to this event tonight fully expecting she'd mortify him, and he planned not to care. How could she not love him?

But if she didn't do something soon, she was going to cry all over him and tell him she loved him, and that was a really bad idea.

So instead she fell forward onto her arms and moved her hips slowly, up and back again, her moisture lubricating his penis so her body slid faster, becoming more and more aroused by the feel of his hard heat between her legs.

"Oh. Man. That is— I—" Ames lifted his head, let it fall back with a cross between a sigh and a groan, obviously giving up on communication. "Yeah."

Eva grinned, tears no longer threatening. They were good together. The best. They'd do okay tonight. And tomorrow. The rest she'd worry about later.

She pushed up off her arms and sat upright, still rocking, stroking her breasts gently, letting him watch her play.

"Come here." He took her hips and maneuvered her forward until she was straddling his head.

"Well." She looked down at him, struggling not to smile. "What now?"

His eyes were fixed on her sex, hovering over his mouth. "I can only think of one thing."

"Really?" She lowered herself slowly, half an inch at a time, making him wait. "This?"

He made an inarticulate sound, grabbed her hips and pulled her down onto his mouth.

Eva drew in a sharp breath between her teeth and let it out on a soft cry, continuing to stroke her breasts while he licked and sucked her ravenously, focusing his attention more and more on her clitoris. Her breathing became labored and harsh. Her thighs started trembling.

The orgasm grew slowly. Eva clutched his hair, eyes closed, head lolling back, barely aware of what she was doing, where she was. Ames's lips closed firmly around her clitoris; he slid a finger up inside her, and she was gone with a guttural shout and the delicious burn that pushed her up, then let her down, while she contracted wildly around his fingers.

"Ames." She moved off him, collapsed to the floor next to him. "Ames, I think you broke me."

"Yeah?" He scrabbled around on the carpet, found a condom somewhere and rolled it onto his still enormous erection. "May I try to fix you?"

"With *that?*" She pointed in pretend horror.

"Well, of course. It's my very best tool."

"Argh! You will have to pay for that horrible pun!" She spread her legs open, arms equally open, inviting him. "Come take your punishment."

"Like a man, I will." He lay over her, his face suddenly serious, ran his hands through her hair, coming up with a still-clinging seal. "You are beautiful, Eva. Amazing. I'm crazy about you."

I love you. Her arms went around his neck; he entered her slowly. They made love with gentle rocking, gazing into each other's eyes, until the feeling was so intense she had to close hers. How could she leave this man? But she couldn't stay. Not only was California her home, but Chris would be wanting her life and her shop back.

"Eva." Her name brought her back. Ames was pushing harder now, breathing harder. He was on his way to coming, and she wanted to be there with him.

Tilting her pelvis up to create more friction, she bore down hard on him, answering each thrust.

"Eva." He held her tightly, muscles straining in his neck and shoulders as his body worked. "You are going to make me come so hard I might break you again."

"Go ahead," she whispered. "Try."

A sharp breath turned into a groan and then a shout as his jaw tightened, his thrusts became fierce and fast, then stopped as he came inside her.

They lay panting for a long while, arms wrapped around each other. Eva refused to allow any thoughts to enter her mind but immense satisfaction, thorough enjoyment of his warm body pressed against hers.

Finally, Ames lifted his head and glanced at the clock over the fireplace. "I hate to say this, but we should probably get dressed."

"Yes." She loosened her grip, all the complicated thoughts flooding back. All they had to face, tonight and in the next week.

"Did I break you?" His touch on her face was achingly tender.

"No." She forced a smile, ran her fingers through his thick soft hair. No, he hadn't broken her body. But after tonight there was no more uncertainty. It was totally within his power to break her heart.

13

AMES WAITED IN the living room, fully dressed, pacing. Yes, he was nervous. He'd committed himself to taking Eva to the dinner and he had no regrets, nothing but certainty that he'd done the right thing, for her and for himself.

How his boss, Mr. Boyce, would take Eva was another matter. Ames didn't like his boss's ultraconservative attitude toward dress and behavior, but he understood it was part of business, living up to the revered decades-old corporate image of neat, professional appearance as well as integrity of action.

Nothing said Ames couldn't become involved with a woman outside Boyce's narrow definition of what passed for appropriate around clients. It was just that no one else in the company had. Besides the annual client dinner, the only place Ames had seen such elegant gowns was on the red carpet in Hollywood. Total waste of time and money to his way of thinking, but that's how it was. When he met Eva it had seemed impossible he'd ever be escorting her to an event like this, but for different reasons than the ones he still worried about tonight. Back then he'd worried only about being embarrassed by her. Now he was worried she'd be treated poorly, snubbed, looked down at, whispered about. And that if that happened, he'd lose his cool and cause some kind of scene. He'd already proved to himself over the drunk harassing her that Eva brought out some pretty fierce protective emotions in him.

Not ingredients that promised a calm evening.

For his part, he'd made as much of a concession as he could, given the wardrobe limits for men. He'd gone out and bought a tuxedo with a Mandarin collar, not exactly wildly rebellious, but definitely not what other guys at the dinner would be wearing. He'd also kept in his earring, which he never wore for business.

Maybe he was worrying for nothing. Maybe no one would even blink at Eva's hair and outrageous clothes. But this was the least he could do to support her, to show her he cared, that she was worth it.

He paced again, glanced at his watch. Again. Where was she? Would she be wearing a plaid skirt with a glittering striped top and gold lamé platform sneakers?

Ames grinned. Now that would be something. He would love to see Mrs. Boyce's face.

The door to the guest room opened—Eva had insisted on dressing in private.

"Ready?" He kept his voice calm and cheerful, waiting for her to appear.

She appeared.

Ames's jaw dropped. He looked her over slowly, top to bottom, bottom to top, and just to make sure he was seeing what he thought he was seeing, top to bottom again.

She was absolutely beautiful, in a little black dress, hair pulled back in a sleek whatever-it-was-called, and a sexy tiny hat-thing with feathers.

Beautiful, and flawlessly, stupendously, amazingly… normal. "Eva." His voice came out low and thick. "You look incredible."

"Think so?" She patted her skirt, clearly pleased by his reaction.

"I'm blown away."

"Yeah?" Her smile dazzled him. She was…perfect. For the dinner. And for him.

"You look handsome, too." She moved toward him, not her usual loose-limbed gait, but precise, model-worthy steps in high black evening sandals. "I love that tux. Not quite regulation, you rebel. You did that for me, didn't you?"

"Sort of." He was humbled by her, her eyes shining in gratitude when it was he who was incredibly grateful. She'd done this for him. So she wouldn't embarrass him. So she'd fit in. She'd suppressed her natural impulse to stand out in a crowd.

For him.

"You didn't have to do this, Eva."

"Do what?" She blinked innocently.

He rolled his eyes. "But I want you to know how much I appreciate it."

"You're welcome."

"And I want you to know that if you had shown up in Lady Gaga's dress made out of meat, I still would have taken you to the dinner proudly."

"Including all the dogs and cats who followed me into the restaurant?"

"Them, too!"

"That means a lot to me, Ames." She giggled, but her eyes were glowing with sincerity and affection…and more? He hoped so. He desperately hoped so. Though what they were going to do about these growing feelings if she was leaving next week…

"Let's go." He offered her his arm, heart bursting with pride, and a certain amount of relief, yes—he was only human. This dinner wouldn't make or break his career, but he hadn't been looking forward to making it a battleground.

They took a taxi to La Grenouille Laide, on Fifty-First Street near Seventh Avenue, holding hands. Tightly. Not speaking much. When had he ever known Eva to be this quiet? He was annoyed at himself for putting her through this.

"It's not going to be that bad."

"No, no, I know." She smiled bravely, which made his heart flip over in his chest. He wanted to tell her she didn't have to go, that they could play hooky, get a beer and burger at P.J. Clarke's on Fifty-Fifth and Third.

But this evening was important to them as a couple. No question, his feelings for Eva were deepening, becoming more and more significant. But if they couldn't navigate each other's worlds, their relationship would eventually be doomed to isolation and lack of communication. While opposites attracting made for romantic press, there had to be some common ground and understanding or they could end up circling each other without a true connection.

Really, no pressure, though.

The cab pulled up at the restaurant. Ames paid the driver, got out and offered a hand to Eva, who took it and emerged from the cab with effortless controlled grace. Who was this woman? She was fantastic. She could even walk naturally on high, spiky heels, one of those mysterious female talents men would never understand.

"Ready?" He offered her his arm to walk into the restaurant.

Her smile was demure. She inclined her head graciously and took his arm. "Never in a million years."

A snort of laughter escaped him before he could get his poker face on. *"Très bien, mademoiselle. Allons-y."*

"Ah, oui, blah, blah, blah!"

Giggling, they marched into the restaurant, a relaxed and elegant room in gold, beige and cream with well-spaced tables and waitstaff as far as the eye could see. Ames identified himself to the maître d', who pointed them toward a back room.

Inside, the usual crowd, gowned and jeweled, suited or tuxedoed.

"My, how the masses sparkle," he murmured to Eva.

"Please don't refer to them as the masses. They hate that," she whispered back.

"Champagne?" A waiter swooped by with a tray, then swooped away.

"Cheers." Ames clinked glasses with Eva and led her over to meet his boss.

Mr. Boyce loved her. Mrs. Boyce loved her. His clients loved her. And why not? She was polite, charming, listened well, asked good questions and reacted in ways that made her conversation partners feel important and interesting.

During the excellent dinner, she used all the right silverware from the bewildering array, sipped and commented on the wines with intelligence and perceptiveness clearly stemming from her vast experience smelling, tasting and judging coffees. She could even use some of the wine crowd's favorite vocabulary—mouthfeel, acidity, finish; clean, buttery, grassy, fruity; chocolate, earth, tobacco—with clear authority.

He was damned impressed. More so when she turned the tables on these wine experts and talked about the coffee-roasting process, taking them from the natural green bean through different stages, defined by visual cues and temperature and sound—the lighter roasts, cinnamon, New England and American to the medium roasts, City, Full City and Vienna, to the dark roasts, French, Italian and finally Spanish—discussing the changes in flavor.

She was a hit. He'd had nothing to worry about, and felt ashamed and embarrassed that he ever had been— except that like all couples, they were learning about each other by encountering different circumstances together.

The most ironic part of the evening was that after all that worry, Ames missed the Eva he knew. He felt as if he'd forced her to crawl into a little box without enough air. He wanted to see her eyes sparkle with enthusiasm, to see her jump up and suggest a game of musical chairs or a group trip to a karaoke bar. *Come on everyone, let's party!*

He loved her. Her spirit, her liveliness and that endless sense of fun. And he wanted a serious shot at finding out what they could be together.

How, he had no idea. Unless his company started selling wines from central California, he'd have very little opportunity to visit her. And her job didn't allow for extensive travel.

How long could you keep up a serious relationship on Skype?

More to the point, who would *want* a serious relationship on Skype? It would be one thing if one or the other of them was planning to relocate, and keeping in touch by phone and computer was a second-best stopgap measure. But they didn't know each other well enough to make such a major decision. And they were already running out of time.

He'd have to let this woman go.

Immediately, rage filled him, along with determination. No. No way. He wasn't going to give up that easily on something so precious and promising.

A few couples got up to leave. Ames put his hand on Eva's back to get her attention, loving the intimacy of touching her. "Ready to go?"

She turned to him, flushed, eyes sparkling brilliantly. "About three hours ago."

He chuckled and kissed her. "I owe you. Let's go home."

"Okay." She blinked sweetly. "Can we do naughty things to each other?"

"Oh, yes. Yes, we definitely can. Let's go *now*." Grabbing her hand, he stood and murmured polite words to the couples seated near them, then pulled Eva over to say good-night and thank-you to the Boyces before he touched base with a few important clients. Then he dragged her down toward Seventh Avenue to hail a taxi home.

A block from the restaurant, practically running to keep up with him, Eva tore off her fascinator and shook out her hair, letting the long waves shine under the street-lights.

"I feel so free!"

He laughed in delight, picked her up and swung her around. "You are the best and most fabulous woman in the world. I can't begin to tell you how wonderful you were in there."

Eva shrugged, clearly giddy with relief. "I just imitated Chris and Natalie and all those hot, perfect women you should be with."

"I'm with the right woman, Eva." He kissed her, not feeling playful anymore. "After tonight I'm more sure than ever."

She put her hands on her hips, looking thoroughly annoyed. "For God's sake, you're not proposing, are you?"

"Ha!" He picked her up and ran with her, a rush of adrenaline giving him the strength of ten thousand men. *"No, I'm not proposing, Eva, my love!"*

She shrieked with laughter. *"Thank God for that, my dearest darling!"*

He put her down, grinning at amused pedestrians. They crossed the street, and he hailed a cab. The city was theirs tonight, the air mild, the night young. But all he wanted to do was get Eva home and show her how he felt about her.

You know, in a guy way.

A cab stopped, and they crawled in, still breathless. Ames gave his address to the cab driver, who grunted and pulled out into traffic.

He wrapped his arm around Eva's shoulders. "You know, it never occurred to me how similar our businesses are until I heard you teaching those people a thing or two about tasting."

"Those people?" she scoffed. "I taught them nothing. My sister or my dad could *really* blow their minds."

He pulled her closer. "You were great."

"Yeah?" She kissed him. "I can go back and put on my clown suits again now?"

"Only if they're low cut and slit up to about—" he put his hand on her thigh, which was so warm and firm he decided it would be criminal not to keep touching it "—here."

"You'd like that?"

"I would." He held her gaze, sliding his hand up her black stockings, which he was extremely happy to discover when his fingers encountered soft skin, turned out to be thigh-highs. He kept his hand moving, loving the way her body grew tense, waiting, her eyes dark and expectant on his.

And then the joke was on him. And on everyone at the party who thought she was a proper and refined young woman.

She wasn't wearing panties.

His cock hardened. He wanted to haul her onto his lap and thrust up into her, watching her get closer and closer to coming, steaming up the windows while the cab driver kept his eyes on the road and the city went on around them.

Eva gasped as his fingers explored her. She was soft, warm and wet. His erection grew painful.

"I think you're going to kill me, Eva."

"That would be unfortunate," she whispered. "Because I really want you to keep touching me."

He groaned. "Just try and stop—"

"Hey! Are youse gettin' outta my cab or what?"

Ames jumped, whipping his hand back into his lap. Eva clapped her hand over her mouth and fumbled for the door, suppressed giggles escaping.

"Uh, yeah." Ames pulled out his wallet and handed over some bills. "Sorry about that."

"Jeez." The driver handed back change, muttering something Ames was not even curious to hear.

He joined Eva on the sidewalk and took her hand. "See what you do to me? I have never in my life forgotten to get out of a cab."

"Gosh, I feel *so* bad." She rolled her eyes, making him smile. He loved that she kept him from taking himself— and his life—too seriously, that she could find the fun in any situation, no matter how embarrassing.

Inside the building, he was deeply disappointed to find someone else waiting for the elevator, since he'd just started a great fantasy involving Eva up against the wall on their way to his floor.

Though he'd probably forget to get off the elevator, too.

However, as soon as the doors opened, they were out, turning to each other, then stumbling down the empty hallway, kissing frantically, Ames struggling out of his jacket. Inside his apartment they left a path of clothes to his darkened bedroom.

Nearly to his bedroom. There was still that elevator fantasy in the back of his mind…

He stopped them at the door, flung off his last piece of clothing, and rolled on the condom he'd stashed in his tuxedo pants just in case. He lunged for Eva and lifted her delicious warm and naked body to his, cupping her bottom, pressing her against the door as she wrapped her strong legs around him and slid her arms around his neck, holding tight, taking some of her weight off his arms.

Totally hot.

After a few giggling tries—her giggles, his frustration—somehow he managed to push inside her.

Her laughter died. His eyes practically rolled back in his head. She was so tight. He thrust into her powerfully, making her body heave up and down and the door bang repeatedly against the wall.

Even hotter.

Eva gave a muted yell, her head lolling to the side, hair cascading down, lips parted, breath coming fast, so beautiful in the dim light. He felt a surge of animal lust and something so much deeper: *my woman.* He widened his stance and pushed harder, responding to an illogical need to leave his print on her, his mark of possession.

Eva gave a yell, then another, and he felt her body gathering. Her eyes shot wide, her mouth opened and she jerked her head back, exposing her long throat as her muscles played his cock, and she nearly screamed her orgasm.

He came immediately in response, slammed into her once and held, shouting as ecstasy took him over.

Oh, man. What had this woman done to him? He'd never experienced anything that primal, that urgent, had never lost himself so completely.

Still panting from the effort and emotion, Ames let her legs slide to the floor. "Did I break you that time?"

"No. Still no." She put her hand to her chest to slow her breathing. "But good try. Keep at it."

"Thanks." He caught up her hand, led her to his bed, disposed of the condom and joined her lying on top of the bedspread, his arms around her, her head fitting just right on his shoulder, her hand resting on his chest.

It didn't get much better than this.

Actually, it could. It could get much better. "I've been wondering."

"Mmm?"

He loved her like this, relaxed and contented. But this was the right time to talk. Things had changed between them tonight, on a lot of levels. "Did you change your flight yet so you can stay longer?"

Eva yawned. "Gee, not yet."

He rolled to his side so he could see her face, what little he could in the light traveling from the living room. "Would you consider it?"

She stiffened. "Wait, are you serious?"

"Yes." He stroked the hair at her temple, following it down the curve of her head, down to her neck and the hummingbird tattoo. "I want more time with you. I want to see where we can go."

I love you.

The words stuck in his throat. He was ready to say them. What else could these crazy, intense feelings be? What else could the quiet, sure ones be? What more did he want than a beautiful woman who challenged his vision of himself and who made him laugh and who fit into his life so well? Who made him play mini golf!

But he wasn't sure she was ready to hear them.

"I'd like that, too." She laid her hand on his cheek. "I've never had this much fun with anyone."

Ames tried not to cringe. *Fun?* He was in love with her and she was having fun? He couldn't quite believe that. "But…?"

"Well, for one thing, Chris will want to come back."

"Are you sure? Has she said she's anxious to come home?"

"No." Eva frowned. "She said she's having a blast."

"Ah." He kept stroking Eva's hair, feeling panic rising. She wasn't exactly jumping up to call her sister. "Would you ask her if she wants to stay longer? Just to find out?"

"I don't know." She moved restlessly onto her back, farther away from him, leaving cold skin where she'd been pressed to his side. "I guess I figure, okay, so, what if we get more time together? How much, a week? A month? Then what? It's not like anything major can change."

Ames's panic increased. He forced it back, breathing deeply. "We could get pretty serious about each other."

Her breath went in with a rush. "Ames…"

"Hey, don't freak out." He kept his voice light. "Anything's possible."

She giggled unconvincingly. "It is, I know."

"Will you call Chris and ask her?"

Her eyes went wide. He could see the pain in them, the fear.

"Ames. I…really don't think I can."

His heart sank, his chest tightened—only a fragment of the pain that was coming, he knew instinctively.

No matter how deeply she felt about him, it wasn't going to make a difference.

Fun-loving Eva still just wanted fun.

14

WAS IT RUDE to tell your wildly happy roommate and her equally delirious boyfriend to shut the hell up?

Eva lay on Chris's bed, one arm dangling over the side of the mattress, the other bent resting over her face.

Giggle, giggle. Talk, talk. And the worst? The silences.

Spit was being mingled.

Disgusting.

She hoped they both came down with severe cases of—

No, she didn't. She was happy for Natalie and Tom, genuinely happy. And also whiny and envious. But Eva's time would come. Maybe Mr. Right would walk into Slow Pour the day she got back. Or she'd sit next to him on the plane next week. Or maybe she'd coast through another year and a half and marry Zac. Their life together would be fun and easy. After knowing Ames, she could now see how there would always be something missing. But at least Eva had discovered an important part of her character during this past month.

She could fall in love.

And she couldn't handle it.

Why? Where had this defect come from? Who knew? Maybe she should go into therapy and see if she could dig up some reason. Her parents hadn't had the most passionate relationship, but they were certainly fond of each other and seemed content. Maybe like her—before she knew Ames—they'd never stumbled over a deeper love. Or maybe they had. Maybe they'd met other people earlier in their lives who set their souls on fire and had sensibly known to avoid the perils of burning up too quickly. In that case, Eva would for once be the apple who'd stayed near the tree.

Either way, didn't matter. When Ames had been talking about Eva staying in New York past the appointed date, she'd frozen like a cornered animal, instinct screaming *no, no, no, no!* What could she do? Her instinct was a good deal wiser than she was and she'd always trusted it before this. Why stop now?

Poor Ames. She didn't want to hurt him. She adored him! Being able to accompany him last night into that totally intimidating restaurant peopled by totally intimidating glitterati, and not only manage but do really well, connect with people and not embarrass him or herself—she'd been giddy. And grateful for the chance to prove to them, and most of all to herself, that she was not the sum of her outfits. Back at Ames's condo, she'd been madly in love and on top of the world.

Until he'd asked her to stay longer. And the world had bucked her off. Obviously she'd been kidding herself that she might have changed. Chris was right. Love was still a game to her. Life was a game to her. She wasn't cut out for a serious, passionate and intimate relationship, no matter how different her feelings for Ames had seemed.

Her cell rang on the mattress next to her. Chris.

Oh, no. Talking to her sister would just torture her with reminders of her cowardice and failings. She'd told Ames she couldn't even ask if Chris had any interest in staying longer in Carmia. It was beyond her. Even for another few weeks. Even to please a man she'd thought she was in love with. Even though her sister would probably say no and the whole thing would be a nonissue.

Eva answered the call. She'd talk to Chris. She wasn't *that* pathetic. She hoped.

"Hey, Chris."

"Hey…you napping?"

"No."

"Sick?"

"No."

"In that case, I'm worried. What is happening?"

"Oh, nothing. I crushed Ames's heart last night and I feel like a total jerk."

Her sister gasped. "Oh, no, Eva. The dinner was a disaster?"

"No." Eva laughed bitterly. Oh, the irony. "The dinner was a fabulous success. I dressed appropriately and talked coffee the way they talk wine and we all got along fine."

"Fabulous, good for you! I bet Ames was happy… Wait, but now apparently he's not?"

"Nope."

Chris started whistling a random tune. "Seriously, any time you want to tell me is fine, I'll just amuse myself here alone until you do."

Eva sighed and rolled over onto her stomach, cheek resting on the bedspread. "I need to work up the courage. Tell me what's going on with you first."

"Oh. I don't know if you want to hear it."

"Of course I want to hear it!" Eva wrinkled her nose. Unless her sister was about to say she was marrying Gus.

"So, Gus—you remember Gus."

Eva barely stopped herself from groaning, calculating how fast she could fly out and stage an intervention. "Ye-e-e-s?"

"Well, he has this friend. A kind of mentor, really. Surfing and all that."

"Oh?" Eva propped herself up on one elbow, pleased that even in her pitiful-me state, she could still be excited for her sister. "That totally gorgeous guy, a little older than we are, what's his name?"

"Bodie?"

"Yes!" Eva's eyes shot wide. That was some serious piece of man. "You landed *Bodie?*"

"No, no, nothing that exciting. I just met him. But I'm going to see him again."

"Wow." Bodie was like… He was…well, he was a complete *zero* compared to Ames, of course, but whoa. Hot. "You're going to have to hurry to start something. That sucks that you met him so late in the month!"

"Oh. Yeah. So…"

Eva frowned. Something was making her sister very uncomfortable. "So?"

"I was so sure this was a good idea, something you'd jump at. But if Ames has his heart crushed, that means things aren't going well between you two."

"What does Bodie have to do with Ames? You are confusing me."

"Yes. Okay." She took a deep breath. "I just have to say it. Eva, I was wondering…"

Silence.

"Oh, Chri-i-i-s, I'm still he-e-e-re."

"I thought maybe you'd want to stay in New York longer. I mean, keep the switch going for a while longer. Like a month. Or…sort of indefinite. Maybe month by month. Or maybe…" She paused for breath after the rush of words. "Well, what do you think?"

Eva got off the bed and stood with her mouth wide open until she caught sight of herself in Chris's mirror on the wall and realized she looked like an idiot. "I can't believe you just said that."

"Oh, honey. I didn't think it would upset you that much. I'm sorry. Forget it. I'll put on my big-girl pants and come home as planned."

"No, no." Eva started to pace the tiny room, hand to her temple. "It's not that. It's that…Ames asked me the same thing last night. To stay longer."

Predictable gasp. "No way. But then, if his heart is crushed, that means you—"

"Shot him down."

"For my sake? Because if that's the case, there's no problem anymore since—"

"Not because of you."

"Oh, Eva, why?" Her sister was clearly distressed. "I thought you were really into him."

"I am!" She lifted her hand, let it fall, spun around and hit her knee on the dresser, then collapsed onto the bed, rubbing it. *Ow, ow, ow.* "I just, I don't know, panicked or something."

"How do you feel this morning?"

She groaned. "Horrible."

"Because you see now that you made the wrong decision shooting him down?" Chris sounded ridiculously hopeful, which made Eva feel ridiculously worse.

"I didn't exactly jump at the idea when you brought it up, either."

"Right. I'm so sorry, Eva."

"No, I'm sorry." A siren sounded outside. Eva pressed the phone harder to her ear so she could hear. "I'm letting you down, too, because you want to stay."

"No, no. Look. We had a deal, you're honoring it, and I will, too. This was a pipe dream for me because I thought you'd want to stay with Ames. It was just a chance to have wild insane sex with a guy whose body could start its own religion."

"Argh! Can't you just have a crazed affair for the next week?"

"Bodie's out of town. Competing. Back the day after I leave."

"Oh." Miserable silence. Miserable Meyerses. Eva had now disappointed her two favorite people in the world. Maybe she should call Zac to see how she could disappoint him, too. Then her parents. Kindergarten teacher after that? "Let me think about it for a while, Chris."

"No. Seriously. This was a completely ridiculous idea. I miss New York and I'll be fine. I'll change my hair or something."

Eva laughed and ended the call, wishing her sister love, wishing she could hit Rewind and do this month over. She'd avoid Ames, and not—

No, she would never do that. As much as this hurt, she would never wish she hadn't met him, hadn't gotten to know him, hadn't fallen in love with him.

She flopped back down onto Chris's bed, buried her face into the pillow. Outside the squeal of tires and angry honking, then furious obscenity-laden shouts. Down the hall, icky sex noises.

Eva grabbed the pillow and put it over her head, screwing her eyes shut. She missed California. The wide-open space, the quiet, the slower pace of life. She missed her privacy. She missed her bed.

She imagined herself lying in it, windows wide-open, the sound of the surf coming through clearly, Ames's arms around her... *Mmm.*

Wait. How did he get there? He lived here.

She adjusted the pillow and went back to California,

strolling Aura Beach at sunset, letting the waves splash her ankles, her hand in Ames's…blissful.

Her eyes opened. Him again. In California. Again.

Wait a second…

She slithered off the bed and onto the floor, got in lotus position, cleared her mind, relaxed her body, concentrated on her breathing. In a few minutes she fell into the familiar light trance of meditation, and imagined herself staying with Ames in New York. Together at another client dinner. Eating falafel on a bench in Washington Square Park. Playing mini golf. Serving him coffee at NYEspresso.

The inner voice was clear as a bell, same as ever, *no, no, no, no.*

She regrouped, redirected, refocused. Went back to California. With Ames. Again strolling on the beach, picnicking at the cliffside table, serving him coffee at Slow Pour. Introducing him to Zac…

Yes.

Adrenaline poured through her system. She got to her feet, breathing hard, her chest heaving.

It wasn't Ames she didn't belong with.

It was New York.

AMES SAT AT his desk, staring at the phone. He had about ten calls to make. Existing clients. Potential clients. Vineyards they worked with. Vineyards they wanted to work with.

He didn't want to talk to anyone.

How could one woman rule his life to this extent? He'd never been this caught up in anyone, never had a woman who wielded this much power over him without any attempt on her part to do so.

Maybe he should have known from the beginning

Eva would be trouble, when she'd approached him in NYEspresso with his armful of flowers for her sister and told him she'd like to order him for home delivery.

The memory stabbed him. How had he gone from exasperation with her to giddy heights of passion and love, then down to the painful depths in such a short time?

If this was what love did, maybe he should give it up. Maybe Eva was right to be so afraid of letting herself fall—he was sure that was the problem. Not that she didn't or couldn't love him, but that she felt it would squash her as flat as the little black dress.

He wanted her to stay as she was, colorful and free. But with him.

Of course it was too much to ask her to give up her life in California for him. But another month…was that too much? Or was she right and whether she stayed or went, they'd still be stuck in this same place?

"You know, I've seen misery in my life, but nothing as depressing as being around you."

He tried to hide how badly she'd startled him. "Yeah, thanks, Jean. That was really sweet."

"I'm serious." She folded her arms across her Yankees sweatshirt and glared at him through her thick glasses. "You're a loser."

"Really. I'm a loser. Hey, thanks again."

"You're welcome. Dinner is in the refrigerator—I made you chicken soup—see if it will make you feel any better." She rolled her eyes. "Though I doubt it."

He nodded, reaching for the phone, even though he had no intention of talking to anyone. He just wanted her to leave. "Thanks, Jean. You can—"

"Only one thing good for what ails you, buddy."

"Yeah?" He took a breath, started counting to ten.

"Grow a pair."

That was it. *"Excuse me?"*

"I said—"

"Yeah, I heard you."

"You miss her? You love her? Go after her!"

He laughed humorlessly. "Yeah, it's not quite that sim—"

"Sure it's that simple." She jammed her hands on her narrow hips. "I told my husband no for six months. Did he give up? Did he sit in his office doing the big boohoo? No. He kept coming over and he kept asking."

"Look, I'm not inter—"

"Look how Eva got *you!*" Jean gestured contemptuously at him. "She just kept coming over. Did you want to see her? No! Did you think she was a pain in the ass? Maybe a little. But then you fell in love with her. I helped her because I looked at her and I said, that girl is in love with Ames the way my Manny was with me. He still is, in fact, in case you were wondering."

"I wasn't." He rubbed his forehead irritably, wanting to talk about Eva about as much as he didn't want to. "If she was in love with me, she wouldn't be running back to California as fast as possible."

"Says you. You know nothing." Jean marched up to the edge of his desk and shook her finger at him. "You wouldn't know love if it was a herring that slapped you across the face."

He stared incredulously. "A *what?*"

"You ever been slapped in the face with a herring, Ames? Well, I have. And I'm telling you—" She broke into a giggle and fanned at her face. "Okay, okay, I lied about the herring."

"What the—" He chuckled unwillingly. "Jean, for God's sake."

"What can I say? I got carried away. Get over it."

"Is this going to take much longer?" He pointed to a pile of folders on his desk. Untouched since an hour ago when he sat down after lunch. "I have work to do."

"Of course you do. You gotta get yourself out from behind this desk and go after her. Every day. And if she goes back to California, you pick up, you sublet this place, rent an apartment near her, and show up. Every day. If you have to sell wine to stay alive, sell California wine. They got plenty out there."

He stared at her. Blinked. Stared some more. Why the *hell* didn't he think of that?

Because he was strictly an in-the-box thinker, a non-spontaneous non–risk taker, which was why Eva had intrigued and irritated and enchanted him so much from the first day her met her. Because part of him undoubtedly wanted to *be* her.

His mind started spinning slowly, then faster and faster until his thoughts were as chaotic as his emotions.

When was the last time he'd taken a vacation? He must have a few weeks coming anyway. He could try out California. There was no shortage of wine in the state. He had fantastic contacts here and abroad, good experience…

The thoughts stalled. What the hell? This was crazy thinking. He wasn't the type to pick up and move on a whim. Away from friends? Away from family? Away from *New York?*

The apartment phone rang.

"I got it." Jean went to answer.

Ames stayed at his desk, tempted to lock his office door so she couldn't get back in and lecture him more on what a loser he was, except that would be a total loser thing to do.

Going after Eva every day was a lovely concept for a movie, but it was dangerously close to stalker behavior.

No meant no, and if she didn't want to stay for him now, dangling himself in front of her, pleading, wasn't likely to change her mind. He'd groveled plenty already and she'd given him a firm, well-thought-out answer.

Subject closed.

"Uh. Ames?" Jean was at the door, phone in hand, looking incredulous. "I keep telling Frank there's some mistake, but he won't budge."

His heart launched into triple time. Had Eva shown up? Changed her mind? "What is it?"

"He says your gorilla is here."

Aw, jeez. *Sure, go ahead—kick a man while he's down.* Ames had ordered the statue two weeks ago, along with a miniature putting green to put in the corner of his living room that Eva said needed brightening with exactly those two things. There had been a delay in the order, then in all the mess, he'd forgotten about it.

What the hell had he been thinking? What was he going to do with a—

He was suddenly was able to hear himself. *No,* he wasn't going to go after her, *no,* he wasn't going to move to California, *no,* he wasn't going to take a vacation, *no,* he could no longer handle a life-size gorilla, *no, no, no...*

Jean was right.

Ames was a loser.

He kept his expression serious. "Well, it's about time."

"You're kidding. Tell me you're kidding."

"Jean." He spoke patiently. "Every apartment needs a gorilla. This one is mine."

She looked at him in concern. "Does this mean you've finally lost it?"

"Not at all." He pushed his chair back, came around the front of his desk, not even in the mood to pretend to work anymore. "I've become a collector of animal statues and small putting greens. This is only the first one. Next, a giraffe. Then a zebra. My living room will become a mini-golf course."

"You are kidding me."

"Am I, Jean?" He perched on the edge of his desk. "Am I really?"

She stared at him suspiciously, then broke into a grin. "Oh, boy. Eva is part of this somehow. I can smell it."

"Could be."

"I shouldn't have doubted you, though, my God, you were acting like a wet blanket. I've seen infants with bigger ones." She put the phone back to her ear. "Send it up, Frank. He definitely wants the gorilla. Yeah. Yeah. I think it's some kind of present for his girlfriend. I know. I don't, either, but kids these days…"

Ames started grinning. He had a feeling he wouldn't stop for quite a while.

"Okay. Your gorilla is on the way." She handed him the phone. "Use it wisely."

"The phone or the gorilla?"

"Yes." She surprised him with a warm hug. "Good luck, Ames. I have a feeling about you and this girl."

"Thanks, Jean. I do, too."

She patted his arm. "Just don't screw this up or you'll be lonely and miserable for the rest of your life."

"Oh, for—" He gave her a big smacking kiss on the cheek. "That is so sweet."

"Hey, they don't call me honey for nothing." She winked. "I lied again. No one calls me that."

"Not surprised."

Jean snorted and started for the door. "Okay, you want me out of here so you can call Eva. Not to worry, I'm going. I'm gone."

"Thanks, Jean. Truly. I'll see you Thursday."

"Only if I live that long." She stopped at the door and turned back to smile, a warm and lovely one he wasn't sure he'd ever seen before. "And you're entirely welcome."

15

Eva glanced at the clock. Again. Who kept turning the hands back? The day couldn't possibly be going this slowly. Her shift ended at two, and then she had somewhere important to be.

In Ames's arms. With her mouth pressed against his, and her eyes devouring the wonderful and sexually irresistible sight of him.

Not that everything would be fixed by her coming back to him. Certainly the agony of the past several days' separation would be behind them, and the uncertainty of her feelings, the fear that she'd never be able to commit to any one man seriously—that would be gone. Eva wasn't defective. She loved Ames. She wanted to be with him forever.

All those issues were fixed and the relief was immense. But getting there had presented her with more problems. She could call Chris, tell her the switch back was off indefinitely, that they should take it month by month, that she'd fallen head over heels in love with Ames and wanted to be with him in New York.

The problem? She didn't want to be in New York. She missed California, she missed her shop, she missed her routines and the peace and the room just to be. What she'd been lacking there on the coast, what she'd needed to cure the boredom that had started this monthlong adventure, wasn't the thrill and excitement of a big city. It was Ames.

And that introduced the next problem. Ames was a New Yorker. Well, she supposed to most New Yorkers, he was Jersey scum, but as far as she was concerned, he fit the city organically and the city fit him. Plus he not only had a job here, but a career, one that afforded him international travel and contact with some of the most creative food and wine minds in the city, and—as a good New Yorker would tell you—therefore the world.

Why would he give that up for her? How could she ask him to?

She couldn't.

And that was why, though she was incredibly impatient to get to his house, to make sure he understood what she was feeling, and how those feelings had driven her actions and decision last time they were together, she was also filled with a sick, doomed certainty that having finally fallen in love with the man of her dreams, their life together until death did them part would stay alive only in her fantasies.

How depressing was that? How could she marry Zac now? She'd been ridiculous even thinking she could settle for less than a wildly passionate and deeply intimate lifelong love affair. She could see now that Zac had mostly been a buffer against her fear that she was unlovable, that this blissful union other people all over the world seemed to slide into regularly was somehow not going to happen to her.

Well, guess what?

"Hey, Eva." Fingers snapped in front of her face. "You in there?"

She jerked back to the present. Tom was standing about a foot away from her, looking amused, Natalie draped all over him, as Natalie was pretty much every time she saw him now. It was lovely, thrilling and just a tiny bit nauseating.

He did look incredibly handsome in his new haircut and new cool clothes. There was still something of a beauty and the beast element to their pairing, but that delighted Eva.

"Oops. Sorry." She stepped over toward him. "I was… thinking about inventory."

"Uh-huh." Natalie shook her head sympathetically. She and Eva had been up late talking the night before. Natalie was in that same la-la land as all couples in the early days of their relationship, thinking nothing was simpler than being happy, and all you had to do was find the guy and everything else would fall into place.

As Eva said, a tiny bit nauseating.

"So what can I get you, coffee and…?"

"Coffee, a latte and your company when you get off work."

Eva grimaced apologetically. "I can get you the first two…but I have somewhere to be."

"Ooh!" Natalie brightened. "Good! Good for you."

Eva winked conspiratorially, thinking what an amazing transformation Natalie had undergone since their first meeting, when she'd barely been able to summon a polite word or a thought that didn't involve herself. She'd simply been unhappy.

Though Tom would definitely have his hands full on occasion. People didn't change *that* completely.

"Tom has some news." She beamed at him. "Tell her."

"My *Importance of Being Earnest* musical has some interest."

Natalie scoffed. "Some interest? Only crazed enthusiasm by one of the biggest Broadway producers in New York, Scott—"

"Shh." Tom's hand went gently across her lips. "No counting chickens."

Natalie rolled her eyes. "Mmgaaffmgrb."

"You are so right." He took his hand off and kissed her cheek. "Thanks for being happy for me."

"Tom!" Eva beamed at them both and handed Tom his coffee. "This is so cool. I will keep my fingers crossed."

"Thanks."

Eva turned to the Beast to pull an espresso shot for Natalie's latte, feeling warm and fuzzy and thrilled for the two of them, and for Tom's success…and also a little envious, and a little bitter, for which she was immediately ashamed. Why did human emotions have to be so complicated?

She'd just finished pouring the foaming milk into Natalie's mug when she heard a gasp behind her and turned.

Another gasp, hers this time, and a wild acceleration of her heart.

Jinx had come in, ready to take over for her. Behind him, a giant bouquet of flowers was walking into the shop. Flowers with male legs.

Really nice legs. Not that you could tell since they were in perfectly pressed beige khakis, but she happened to know that about them.

She heard a mumble of admiration around the shop—business had picked up considerably midmorning and midafternoon since she'd made her little changes.

The flowers, a brilliantly rainbow-colored assortment of blooms large and small, multipetaled and single, tall and short, round and oval and spiky and feathery, delicate and substantial, lowered.

The only thing in the room more beautiful and amazing and heart lifting than the flowers was what had been lurking behind them.

"Wow." Eva pressed her hands to her face, afraid she'd start bawling. "Oh, wow."

"Hi." Ames Cooke was the most gorgeous and amazing man who'd ever lived, she was certain of it. Because he was looking at her as if she was the most gorgeous and amazing woman who ever lived, and that was exactly as it should be when you were madly in love.

"Ames. Those are so beautiful." She blinked demurely. "But, um, you know Chris isn't here…"

"I guess you'll have to keep them." He grinned and set the vase on the corner of the counter. The blaze of glory lit up the shop. A few customers applauded.

"Would you like some coffee?" Her voice came out breathless. She couldn't take her eyes off him, not sure how she'd survived so many days without seeing him. She was starved for him, his scent, his skin—she practically wanted to ingest the poor guy.

All she could hope was that he felt exactly the same. And the way his dark eyes were fixed on her, there was a good chance he did.

"No coffee, thanks. I was hoping you'd be ready to leave soon." He glanced at his watch. "I have an important call at four, but I was wondering if you'd like to—"

"Yes."

He grinned. "Well, okay, then."

"I'll cover you." Jinx laid a hand on Eva's shoulder, making her jump. Were there other people in the world? She'd forgotten. "Don't worry, boss, you go."

"Thanks, Jinx. I'll just clean—"

"Nope." He pointed to the door. "You're out. In another few days I don't work for you anymore, so I can start telling you what to do."

"Don't be too sure about that." She winked at his surprised face and handed him her apron. "Good business today, have fun. And thank you. Truly."

"Name your first kid after me." He grinned and shook Ames's hand. "Even if it's a girl."

"Yeah…okay." She hugged him and went around the counter, wanting to skip and cheer and howl at the sun.

One last look at the flowers and she took the hand Ames offered and followed him outside.

"This was such a surprise, Ames. Though I have to tell you I was coming over after my shift today, whether you liked it or not."

"Yeah?" He grinned at her, swinging their hands, walking so fast she practically had to run.

"Are we in a hurry?"

"Yes."

"Why?"

"I have a surprise to show you. And we need to talk. And I want your clothes off."

"In what order?"

He squeezed her fingers. "Doesn't matter."

They barreled down Forty-Third Street, entered his building, strode through the lobby, Eva barely having time to throw out a breathless, "Hi, Frank," before Ames had dragged her onto the elevator.

The doors closed, and she was in his arms. He was murmuring her name. Her body melted against him, exquisite relief coursing through her system. "Oh, that is so much better."

"Yes." He drew his thumb across her mouth, his eyes warm and serious, causing a massive melt in her heart. "I missed you, Eva."

"Oh, Ames." She shook her head, gazing at him, unable to believe her luck finding someone so wonderful. "I missed you, too."

The elevator doors opened...back onto the lobby. A startled tenant walked in with her tiny dog on a leash, eyeing them peculiarly.

They hadn't pressed the button.

Somehow they made it to Ames's floor before they cracked up, hurrying to get into his apartment, where he drew her into his arms again and was kissing her madly before they got more than six inches across the threshold.

Wonderful kisses, heart-swelling, chest-aching, fabulous kisses, the kind of kisses that felt like forever, because who would ever not want to feel exactly like this?

"Eva." He pressed his forehead to hers, breathing unsteadily. "We need to talk. We have really important things to say to each other, and really serious stuff to face, and I think if we keep kissing right now we'll just have crazed-beast sex, and that's—"

"A great idea, I agree." She pulled off her pink lace shirt, worn over a black-and-white polka-dot camisole that exposed and enhanced a good portion of her breasts.

Which apparently short-circuited his poor male brain, because he could only stand there staring with his tongue hanging out.

Figuratively, thank goodness.

His mental prowess didn't improve when she kicked off her patent-leather mules and pulled down her black miniskirt and pink leggings, leaving her in the camisole and matching black-and-white polka-dot string bikini panties.

Yes, she had dressed with him in mind that morning. Heck, she'd done everything with him in mind since the hour she met him.

"Uh...I...d'uh..."

"Yes, Ames. Don't strain yourself, sweetheart." She led him to his bedroom, where he again took her in his arms, making incoherent growling noises that had her giggling so hard she ruined her big seduction moment, but that made everything else much more special and fun and distinctly Eva and Ames.

She undressed him slowly, covering every inch of newly exposed skin with kisses, bites, tiny licks, letting him know how happy she was to be with him again.

And when he was naked, he took off her panties and camisole, bending to suckle her breasts—one, then the other—while she tipped her head back, stroking his hair, savoring the feel of his warm mouth and tongue.

Then he lifted his head and looked into her eyes, his dark and open and adoring, and her world changed.

Ames was love. He was the reason she had never truly fallen for anyone before. She would stay in New York; she would sell her shop. Who knew what life held—she might make it back to California someday, but it would have to be with him.

"I talked to Chris." She laid her hand against his cheek, feeling the beginnings of the day's stubble on his smooth, firm skin, touching the gold stud in his ear. "I'm staying in New York. For now. And then…forever, if that's what we decide."

"Eva." His breath hissed in; he cupped the back of her head and brought her close, searching her face. "You'd do that for me?"

"Yes." She felt no panic, nothing but certainty that their lives should be lived together. "I love you. And I want to be with you for a really long time."

Another rush of breath. "I love you, too, Eva."

Then they were kissing again, and as deep and meaningful and wonderful as their kisses had been before, these were ten times as important and soul stealing and magical, because they had just become part of each other in an entirely new way.

He led her to the bed, and they clasped each other close for a long while, enjoying the feel of their skin together, touching and stroking, Eva nearly overwhelmed by her own happiness and a deep and satisfying sense of peace. She felt as if she'd been carrying a burden her whole life that had finally been put down exactly where it was meant to be, and now she got to go forward forever without it.

Ames rolled on top of her, and she welcomed him on, spread her legs as he held himself on one arm, took hold of his beautifully hard penis and moved it slowly back and forth, up and down her sex until its tip glistened with her moisture and neither of them could wait any longer.

He pushed inside her, holding her gaze, smiling with happiness she knew was reflected on her own face. They made love slowly, simply, whispering adoringly, kissing languidly, letting the arousal simmer through their bodies until it grew hot of its own accord and the pace of their sexual rhythm and breathing increased. Their bodies communicated lust and longing, love and desire, rising until ecstasy took them both up and over the edge, and then, inevitably, down.

They lay there for several minutes, holding each other close, savoring each other's warmth and nakedness. Eva had no desire to move; she was cocooned in the glow of what they'd just shared.

Except she was really, really thirsty. "I'm parched. Do you want a glass of water?"

"I'll get it." He was half up before he appeared to change his mind. "Actually, that would be great."

"Okay." She wasn't sure what that was about, but he'd

said he had a surprise. Maybe he needed to prepare while she was out of the room.

She scrambled off the bed, walked to the kitchen, got two glasses of water, turned to go back into his room and nearly dropped them.

"Ames?"

"Yeah."

"Uh." Laugher was already bubbling up. "Were you aware that a gorilla has taken up residence in your living room?"

"No way!"

She let the laughter out, heading back to the bedroom. No wonder he'd wanted her to get the water. "He is the perfect addition. Exactly what the room needed!"

He took the glasses from her while she climbed back into bed. "I was also thinking he might look nice in your house."

"Mine?" Eva lowered her water. "You'd give him up to me so soon?"

"Oh, no, I wouldn't do that. I love the big guy."

She stared at him. "You are not making sense."

"You know that call I have at four o'clock?"

"Now you're making less."

"Bear with me." He took the half-drained glass from her and put it on his nightstand, set his own glass next to it. "It's with a winery in central California. They're looking for someone. I have a few more people I'll be talking to next week. Thought I'd fly out there and find out if any of them want to meet me. See, I was sure the woman I love would be on the other side of the country. That wasn't going to work for me."

"Oh, my God, *Ames!*" She threw her arms around him, practically knocking him out of bed. "You'd do that for me?"

He chuckled, holding her close. "I would. You've opened up so many possibilities to me, Eva, that I never would have considered even a few weeks ago. You got me playing mini golf! But that was only the beginning. I feel as if I've been living my life with my head down, watching the sidewalk for cracks and dog poop, you know? Ignoring what's around and above me. You gave me a new, full life, and I want to share it with you."

"Oh, Ames." Tears came into Eva's eyes. She'd never felt this loved or cherished, never dreamed she could inspire this kind of passion and trust in someone who'd inspire the same in her. "You taught me not to be afraid anymore of who I am under these trappings, and what that woman wants. Which, by the way, is you. You have changed my life, too, and you have no idea what that means to me."

"Maybe not." He kissed her, kissed her again. "But whether we end up here or in California, I'm betting we have a lifetime for me to find out."

* * * * *

Eva found her happy ending.
What will happen to her twin sister, Chris,
as the coffee shop switcheroo continues?
Popular author Isabel Sharpe has written
Chris's story, on sale in February 2015
from Harlequin Blaze!

REQUEST YOUR FREE BOOKS!
2 FREE NOVELS PLUS 2 FREE GIFTS!

HARLEQUIN

Blaze®

red-hot reads!

YES! Please send me 2 FREE Harlequin® Blaze™ novels and my 2 FREE gifts (gifts are worth about $10). After receiving them, if I don't wish to receive any more books, I can return the shipping statement marked "cancel." If I don't cancel, I will receive 4 brand-new novels every month and be billed just $4.74 per book in the U.S. or $4.96 per book in Canada. That's a savings of at least 14% off the cover price. It's quite a bargain. Shipping and handling is just 50¢ per book in the U.S. and 75¢ per book in Canada.* I understand that accepting the 2 free books and gifts places me under no obligation to buy anything. I can always return a shipment and cancel at any time. Even if I never buy another book, the two free books and gifts are mine to keep forever.

150/350 HDN F4WC

Name _____ (PLEASE PRINT)

Address _____ Apt. #

City _____ State/Prov. _____ Zip/Postal Code

Signature (if under 18, a parent or guardian must sign)

Mail to the **Harlequin® Reader Service:**
IN U.S.A.: P.O. Box 1867, Buffalo, NY 14240-1867
IN CANADA: P.O. Box 609, Fort Erie, Ontario L2A 5X3

Want to try two free books from another line?
Call 1-800-873-8635 or visit www.ReaderService.com.

* Terms and prices subject to change without notice. Prices do not include applicable taxes. Sales tax applicable in N.Y. Canadian residents will be charged applicable taxes. Offer not valid in Quebec. This offer is limited to one order per household. Not valid for current subscribers to Harlequin Blaze books. All orders subject to credit approval. Credit or debit balances in a customer's account(s) may be offset by any other outstanding balance owed by or to the customer. Please allow 4 to 6 weeks for delivery. Offer available while quantities last.

Your Privacy—The Harlequin® Reader Service is committed to protecting your privacy. Our Privacy Policy is available online at www.ReaderService.com or upon request from the Harlequin Reader Service.

We make a portion of our mailing list available to reputable third parties that offer products we believe may interest you. If you prefer that we not exchange your name with third parties, or if you wish to clarify or modify your communication preferences, please visit us at www.ReaderService.com/consumerschoice or write to us at Harlequin Reader Service Preference Service, P.O. Box 9062, Buffalo, NY 14269. Include your complete name and address.

SPECIAL EXCERPT FROM

HARLEQUIN

New York Times bestselling author
Tawny Weber delivers a sexy new SEAL story.
Here's a sneak peek at

Christmas with a SEAL

The Las Vegas penthouse was a kaleidoscope of sensations. Neon lights glinted off sparkling chandeliers, sending colorful sparkles off the crowd of partiers. Dressed in everything from sequins to plastic, denim to silk, bodies filled the room, covering the leather couches, perching on chrome stools around the bar and flowing onto the dance floor.

Accenting it all were intense music, free-flowing drinks and men. So, so many men.

And, oh, baby, they were gorgeous.

It wasn't just knowing that most of these muscular, sexy men were navy SEALs that made Frankie Silvera's insides dance. It was knowing that somewhere among them was her dream hottie and the answer to all of her problems.

She just had to find him.

"See anything you like?" Lara asked, stepping up beside her.

A room full of sexy guys with smoking-hot bodies?

What wasn't to like?

"I'm here to celebrate your wedding," Frankie said. "Not to hook up."

HBEXP79823

"You're in Las Vegas, Frankie. Go wild. Have fun." Lara laughed as she turned to leave. "Don't forget, what happens in Vegas stays in Vegas."

"Tempting, but I'm not the wild Vegas type," Frankie demurred, keeping her secret dream just that—secret. Frankie wasn't about to share her hope of finding a guy she'd only seen infrequently over the past ten years and seducing him.

Especially not when the guy was Lara's brother.

Taking a second glass of liquid courage that tasted like champagne, she decided it was time to get to work on the best weekend of her life.

Not an easy task. She looked around. There were at least two hundred people here. Figuring it was a gift that all the guys were hot and sexy and made searching fun, she moved through the bodies to cross the room.

Whoa. Frankie narrowed her eyes.

Was that him?

Sitting alone in one booth and looking as if he wanted to be anywhere else, the man was nursing a drink. Mahogany hair, shorn with military precision. A navy blue sweater covered his broad shoulders, emphasizing his perfect posture and, from what she could see, a gorgeous chest.

Lieutenant Phillip Banks.

He was even better looking now. And, oh, my, he was hot.

Nerves danced in her stomach. Frankie bounced in her beribboned heels, wondering if this was what Cinderella had felt like when she'd spotted the prince at the ball.

Half delighted, half terrified.

And totally turned on.

**Pick up CHRISTMAS WITH A SEAL
by Tawny Weber in November 2014
wherever you buy Harlequin® Blaze® books!**

Holiday nights are heating up!

Lucy Vandenburg decides to end her dating dry spell in one naughty, uninhibited night with a sexy stranger. But the man she chooses turns out to be someone she knows all too well....

Don't miss

Oh, Naughty Night!

from *New York Times* bestselling author

Leslie Kelly

Available November 2014
wherever you buy Harlequin Blaze books.